What's in the attic?

Suddenly something sank its teeth into my finger.

I cried out and jerked my hand back. In the dim light, I could see a drop of blood on the end of my forefinger.

"Mom, there's something alive in that box!" I gasped.

My mother crossed the attic toward me. "Must be a mouse," she said with a grimace. "Yuck!" She lifted the dusty box down from the highboy and squinted into it.

"No," she said in a strangely altered voice. "It's not a mouse. It's some kind of animal, but all that's left is its skeleton."

In silence she held out the box.

Books by Ann Hodgman

My Babysitter Has Fangs
My Babysitter Is a Vampire

Available from MINSTREL Books

My Babysitter
Has Fangs

by
Ann Hodgman

Illustrated by
John Pierard

A GLC Book

A MINSTREL® BOOK

PUBLISHED BY POCKET BOOKS

New York London Toronto Sydney Tokyo Singapore

For Lacey McNeal

A MINSTREL PAPERBACK *ORIGINAL*

 A Minstrel Book published by
POCKET BOOKS, a division of Simon & Schuster Inc.
1230 Avenue of the Americas, New York, NY 10020

Special thanks to Ruth Ashby and Pat MacDonald.

Cover painting by Jeffrey Lindberg
Illustrations by John Pierard
Typesetting by Trufont Typographers, Inc.
Developed by Byron Preiss and Daniel Weiss
Editors: Sarah Feldman and Lisa Meltzer
Assistant Editor: Kathy Huck

ISBN: 0-671-75868-3

First Minstrel Books printing July 1992
10 9 8 7 6 5 4 3 2

A MINSTREL BOOK and colophon are registered trademarks of Simon & Schuster Inc.

Printed in the U.S.A.

My Babysitter
Has Fangs

PROLOGUE

I should have paid more attention to the ring. If I had, none of this would have happened.

Of course, maybe it was all *supposed* to happen. And if I hadn't been around, a few people might have ended up—

But I don't want to get ahead of myself. I'll tell the bad part when I get to it. And anyhow, there was no way I could have paid attention to that ring on the first day. If you've ever gone on vacation, you'll know that the first day you arrive someplace there isn't time to pay attention to anything except unpacking.

And there was a *lot* of unpacking to do the day my family and I arrived at our summer house on Moose Island in Maine. Somehow all the luggage we had packed back home in Delaware had had twins or something. My little brother, Trevor, and I (he's going into second grade; I'm going into seventh—and by the way, my name is Meg Swain) had already taken about four million things out of the car, and it wasn't even starting to get empty yet.

As I dragged a nine-hundred-pound suitcase filled with library books out of the back seat, Trevor dumped a pile of beach towels onto the ground and walked around to the front of the car. "Mom, could you get my binoculars?" he asked my mother's rear end. That was all you could see of my mother. The rest of her was stretched out across the front seat trying to coax out our big fat cat, Pooch. Pooch hates anything that involves going anywhere. He had been hiding under the front seat ever since Boston, when he had escaped from his cat carrier.

"Can't you get them yourself?" came my mother's muffled, struggling voice. "Come *on*, Pooch!"

"No, because I don't know where they are," said Trevor calmly. He has a way of not noticing when people are under stress. "Dad packed them, I think."

"Well, in that case, honey—*oof!* Poochie, I *hate* you sometimes!—I think you'd better give up," grunted Mom. "If Dad packed them—what is the matter with this animal? Is he glued to the floor?—anyway, if Dad packed them—ouch, my head!"

From the sound of it, she had just crashed into the glove compartment.

2

"But Mom, what if I see an interesting bird?" my brother persisted. Trevor has gotten very interested in birds recently. (Last year it was dinosaurs.) "I really need my binoculars right—"

"I'll help you find them later, Trev," I broke in hastily. I had a feeling Mom would start yelling if either of us hung around her any longer. "C'mon, let's go bring some of this stuff into the house." I stuffed the pile of beach towels back into Trevor's reluctant arms and began lugging the suitcase of library books toward our front door. The bag clunked against my ankle with every step.

My father had already unlocked the front door and gone down to the basement to look at the fuse box, or whatever it is fathers do down in basements. I dragged the suitcase up the front stoop, walked through the door, and took a deep breath.

The first breath of our summer house! Another great summer on Moose Island was about to begin! I stood there motionless, breathing vacation air in and out. All the scents of summer— the salty sea breeze curling in through the window, the pine trees shading our roof overhead, the musty old summer books and faded *National Geographics* in our living-room bookcase—all those different smells came flooding into my nose's memory. I was so happy to be back!

3

"Meg, why are you panting like that?" asked Trevor from behind me. "You sound like a dog."

I jumped embarrassedly. "Oh, no reason. Here, give me those towels and I'll—"

Then I stopped. Another smell was making its way toward me, and this one wasn't quite as pleasant.

"Mildew! Yuck! Where's that coming from?" I said. "Did the roof leak during the winter?"

Now I *really* sounded like a dog as I sniffed my way across the living room. The smell was coming from the kitchen, and in a second I saw its source: a big pile of clammy, grayish sheets and blankets in a canvas bag under the kitchen table. A thick veil of spiderwebs anchored the bag to the floor.

"Ugh! *Disgusting!*" I shrieked. "We must have forgotten to wash this stuff before we left last year! It's been sitting here for *ten months*, with mice and spiders and stuff crawling in and out! Oh, I'm going to throw up!"

I didn't, though. After I'd carried on a little bit more, I took the bag into the mud room and shoved it and all the stuff inside it into our washing machine. Then I poured in about a quart of detergent and turned on the machine. Don't worry—I checked to see if there were any mice inside the bag first. There weren't.

4

A couple of hours later, when the car was all unpacked and Pooch had finally been coaxed into the house (he was hiding under my bed now), my mother came up to my bedroom with something in her hand.

"I found this in the bottom of the washing machine, honey. Is it yours? I don't think I've seen it before."

She held it out. It was a ring, and I had never seen it before, either. It was pretty, but kind of weird, too—made out of some strange, dark, carved metal with a lot of curlicues that looked almost like some kind of ancient writing. In the ring's center was a smooth oval stone that was such a dull, dark red it was almost black.

It certainly wasn't the kind of thing seventh-grade girls usually wear. Still, I thought it was interesting-looking and maybe even valuable. I didn't see any reason why I shouldn't keep it.

"No, it's not mine," I told Mom, "but I kind of like it. Can I hang onto it until the real owner turns up?"

"Sure, if you want. We'll probably never know whose it was, anyway."

I slipped the ring onto the first finger of my left hand.

Instantly an electric jolt rocked my whole body.

"Ouch!" I yelped.

5

"What's the matter?" asked my mother.

"N-nothing, I guess." I stared at the ring uneasily. It *had* been nothing, right? Rings don't give you electric shocks!

I shoved the ring more securely onto my finger and turned to my mother. "Isn't it about time to hit the beach, Mom? We've been unpacking for hours!"

"That's a perfect idea," said Mom. "I'll go get Dad and Trevor."

So we put on our bathing suits and went down to the beach, and the water was freezing, freezing, freezing cold, and we cooked swordfish and corn on the cob on our grill for supper, and Pooch finally came out from under my bed, and I forgot all about the ring.

Which just goes to show that getting good grades in school doesn't mean you're smart.

CHAPTER ONE

"Meg, Jack is here!" my father called upstairs the next morning.

"What's here? Jack who? Why?" I mumbled. Groggily I rolled over in bed and looked at the clock. It was nine-fifteen. I never sleep that late! Then I realized that I was in the house on Moose Island, and that summer vacation had started—which meant that the Jack downstairs had to be Jack Cornell.

I cleared my throat. "Be right down!" I shouted, hoping my voice didn't sound too sleep-croaky. I jumped out of bed, pulled on my clothes, and ran to the bathroom to brush my teeth. On my way out of the bathroom I luckily happened to catch sight of my hair, which looked as though someone had been knitting with it. I gave it a quick brush—with my hairbrush, of course, not my toothbrush.

I was a little nervous about seeing Jack again. For all the years we've been going to Moose Island, Jack has been my best friend there. (His family lives on the island year-round.) But he's a year older than I am, which meant that this summer he was going into eighth grade. And you know how strange teenage boys can get. I wondered whether Jack had changed a lot, and whether we'd still be friends.

But when I saw him standing at the foot of the stairs, I felt relieved. Except for being a little taller, Jack still looked pretty much the same. He also looked as though my parents were making him feel uncomfortable. That meant he couldn't have gotten *too* mature since I'd last seen him.

"How was your winter, Jack?" my mother was asking. She and Dad were sitting on the sofa reading the paper and drinking coffee.

"It was okay, Mrs. Swain. Or should I say Dr. Swain?" said Jack.

"I'm still Mrs.," Mom told him. "I'll be finished with medical school in a year. *Then* you can call me Doctor."

"You can call *me* Doctor, if you want," my father put in genially. "Screenwriters need all the respect they can get."

Jack smiled politely at this lame joke. "Have you been—uh—writing a lot of screenplays lately, Mr. Swain?" he asked.

"I've just finished one, as a matter of fact," said Dad. "I don't have any big deadlines looming on the horizon. This summer should be a lot easier than last."

Last summer, Mom and Dad were busy every single second, or at least it seemed that way. Mom was working in the emergency room at Moose Island's little medical center, and Dad had a huge deadline. It wasn't much of a vacation for them—or for me and Trevor, either. Luckily things weren't going to be so bad this summer. My mother was writing up the results of some research she'd done over the winter, and Dad was still in what he calls the "proposal stage" of his newest project. That means he has to talk on the phone a lot, but he can put off actually starting to work for ages.

I decided Jack had had enough, and started down. "Ah, here comes Meg," said Dad, turning toward the stairs. "Thudding down the steps like an elephant, as usual."

I rolled my eyes. My father never hesitates to embarrass me when he gets the chance. "Hi, Jack," I said shyly, trying to take the last few stairs more quietly.

"Meg, you slug!" was Jack's reassuring greeting. "How could you oversleep on a day like this? Let's bike over to the public beach." He sounded as though he'd just seen me the day before instead of ten months ago.

"Well, sure, but why?" I was a little startled.

"I mean, why can't we just stay here or go to your house? There are beaches at both places."

"Because I've got a sailing lesson there later," said Jack. "I'm taking sailing every day this summer. It's pitiful how behind I've let myself get compared to the other guys in my class."

"Well, that's . . . nice," I said. "That you're sailing a lot, I mean. Sure, I'll go."

"Can I come, too?" called Trevor from his room upstairs. "I want to feed the seagulls! I have some bread all saved up from home!"

"Of course you can go, honey," Mom called back to him.

"Oh, Mom, does Trev have to come?' I wailed. "He can't start tagging along *already!* The summer's just started!"

My mother gave me a meaningful look. "Now, Meg, you know this is the first year Dad and I are letting you take care of Trevor on your own. We've never thought you were responsible enough before."

"Well, I know, but—"

"So you need practice!" interrupted my mother. "I would think you'd be glad to have your brother's company, anyway. And Trevor certainly isn't old enough to bike to the public beach alone," she finished, as though that were the perfect reason we should take him along.

"Oh, okay," I grumbled. "I'll go change into my bathing suit. Just wait one more second, Jack. *Trev!* You'd better get your suit on fast, or you're not coming!" I shouted crossly up the stairs.

"I've got it on already," yelled my brother. "I slept in it."

We had to bike in single file on the road to the beach, which meant that Jack and I didn't get to talk much on the way. So let me use this space instead to fill you in on all the stuff that happened to me last summer on Moose Island.

You're not going to believe it. I hardly can myself.

First of all, last summer Trevor's and my regular summer babysitter, Libby, went to horseback-riding camp on the mainland. (Wait, that's not the unbelievable part.) Since Mom and Dad wouldn't have dreamed of letting me and Trevor stay in the house alone, they hired another babysitter. His name was Vincent Graver, and he had a job in the blood bank of the medical center where Mom was working.

Vincent wasn't your everyday babysitter. He was . . . I guess I'd better just say it right out: he was a vampire. I know, I know—there's no such thing, and even if there *were,* vampires live in Transylvania, not Maine. Well, I still don't know why Vincent decided to move to Moose Island, but he definitely did do it. And Jack and I had to get rid of him. It took us a long time, and it was pretty terrifying, but we finally succeeded.

You see, vampires have to sleep in the dirt they were buried in. Vincent had been storing the dirt *he* was buried in in his coffin. Jack and I found the coffin and dumped all the dirt from it into a bag and carried the bag to the ferry and dumped the dirt into the ocean. So naturally it got all scattered in the waves, and Vincent threw himself into the water after it, and we never saw him again. (I'm making this all sound a lot easier than it actually was.) Then Libby unexpectedly came back from riding camp early, and the rest of our summer was great.

Just ask Jack about all this if you don't believe me—only you can't, because he's biking along a tricky stretch of road right at this point in the story and he can't talk. You'll have to take my word for it. It almost seems like a dream to me now, but it really did happen.

As I pedaled along behind Jack I felt relieved that this year we'd be having a more ordinary summer. Jack is always telling me what a coward I am, and I guess it's true. I hate adventures. I only like reading about other peoples' adventures, preferably when I'm lying safe in my bed. Biking to a beach I didn't usually visit was plenty of excitement for one day. Jack loves big, complicated adventures. A simple solution to a problem? In Jack's opinion, there's no such thing.

When we reached the beach at last, Trevor threw his bicycle to the ground and rushed to the waterline with his bag of bread. "I've even got some stale brownies!" he called back over his shoulder. "The seagulls are going to love me!"

I grinned. "Moose Island will have the fattest seagulls in Maine," I said to Jack. "You should have seen the way Trevor fed the birds back home. On Valentine's Day he made them a heart-shaped cake out of suet and peanut butter."

"Sounds kind of good," said Jack absently. "Oh, look, there's Sheldon Bradshaw. That guy is such a dip. On the first day of school, he took his . . ."

For the next ten minutes Jack filled me in on all the Moose Island gossip. Then, for the next *one* minute, we went swimming. That was all I could take. At the beginning of the summer, the water is always way too cold for me. It's another reason Jack calls me a coward.

"Well, not too many of the other people here are swimming," I pointed out as we sat back down on our towels again. It was almost lunchtime now, and the beach was starting to fill up with picnickers. At the water's edge, Trevor was feed-ing a frenzied cloud of seagulls who obviously couldn't believe their luck.

"I know, but you could at least *try* to—" Sud-denly Jack broke off. "Look, what's this black sand doing here? It wasn't here before, was it?" He pointed down next to his towel.

A dark, oily-looking streak of black sand was snaking through the ordinary sand like some kind of unpleasant vein.

Jack stirred it with his finger. "Did the tide just bring this in?" He squinted out to sea. "Hey, maybe it's an oil slick!" he said excitedly. "I bet a boat crashed out there! Wow, maybe we'll have to organize a rescue!"

I stared down at the sand myself. And as I did, a very strange feeling suddenly washed over me.

"We've got to leave right away," I suddenly heard myself saying. "We're in danger."

I hardly knew where the words were coming from—but somehow I knew they were true.

"What are you talking about?" asked Jack incredulously.

I jumped to my feet without answering. "Trevor! *Trevor!*" I called. I dashed over to him and grabbed his hand. Pieces of bread showered all over the sand. "Let's go get our bikes," I said breathlessly.

"But I still have some bread left," Trevor protested as I yanked him along.

"It doesn't *matter!*" I yelled.

"But Meg, those poor birds are starving!"

"No, they're not! Anyway, we have to hurry!"

I dragged Trevor past Jack, who was still staring at me in bewilderment. "Come on!" I called to Jack. "Are you crazy?"

"Are *you?*" he said. "I've got a sailing lesson in a few minutes."

"There won't be any lesson today! Believe me!" I was almost screaming, I wanted to get away so badly.

Now Trevor and I had reached the bike rack. Jack was walking a few steps behind us, still arguing with me. Just as Trevor and I climbed onto our bikes, a massive bolt of lightning sizzled through the sky.

"Okay, Meg, I believe you," said Jack quickly. And he scrambled onto his own bicycle as fast as he could.

The loudest thunder I'd ever heard crashed directly over our heads. On the beach, the picnickers began to throw their lunches back into their picnic baskets. The few swimmers still out in the water struggled toward shore.

Torrents of rain began pelting down. And I mean *torrents.* It was just as if someone had

turned on a sky-sized shower. And the wind . . . remember the tornado in *The Wizard of Oz*? That's exactly what the wind sounded like.

I knew we weren't safe out in a storm like this. But we weren't safe on the beach, either. Where could we go except home?

"Pedal hard, Trevor!" I yelled. I wasn't even sure he could hear me over the wind. "Follow Jack! I'm right behind you!"

As the three of us set off in a wavering line, our wheels skidding crazily under that drenching rain, I glanced back over my shoulder.

The ocean was jet-black now. It was churning and frothing like some kind of devil's brew. Towels left behind by their fleeing owners were whipping across the sand, and I saw one forgotten picnic basket tumble end over end until it smashed into a boulder and splintered to bits.

Then the biggest wave I have ever seen in my life reared up over the shore.

I didn't want to see any more. I bent my head into the shrieking wind and pedaled like mad for home.

CHAPTER TWO

An hour later, the storm was still screaming outside. Since *we* weren't outside, though, we didn't care. Wind was tearing around the corners of our house as though it were furious it couldn't get at us, and a raging rain was slapping the windows. But none of it could touch us. Our bikes were safe in the garage, and Trevor and Jack and I were safe in front of a crackling fire, drinking hot chocolate. Actually, the fire was hissing more than it was crackling, because the wood we'd brought in from the garage was sort of wet, thanks to the leak in the roof there. But the three of us were still happy to be where we were.

"Well, this is pretty weird weather, that's all I can say," Jack announced. "There was nothing in the weather forecast about a storm. We were supposed to have great weather for the whole week. I just hope I can go sailing tomorrow. . . . Is there any more hot chocolate left?"

"I'll check." I stretched out my hand for the

kettle, which was resting on the hearth. Then I paused.

"Could you get that, Mom?" I called. "We're all too cozy to move."

"Get what?" my mother called back from the kitchen.

"The phone, of course!"

Just then the telephone rang.

I blinked, confused, and the phone rang again. Its sound made me realize it *hadn't* been ringing before. Then how had I known it was going to?

Jack turned to stare at me. "That's the second time today," he said. "The second time you've guessed something was going to happen before it did. Did you turn psychic over the winter?"

"Yeah, sure," I said with an attempt at a laugh. "I guess I'm just . . . uh . . . lucky. Or something."

No one is really psychic, right? There's always some kind of trick behind those lucky guesses. But over the next few days, I had plenty of chances to wonder whether I *had* somehow developed some kind of weird ability to predict things.

There was the time I passed my father the pepper before he asked for it. (Okay, my father likes lots of pepper on his food, so passing him the pepper is usually a safe bet.)

There was the time I went to comfort Trevor

even before he woke up from his bad dream. (Okay, maybe he was calling out in his sleep and it sort of filtered through into *my* sleep.)

There was the time I told my mother, "I *am* standing up straight!" before she had a chance to say a word. (Okay, I might have caught her eye in the mirror without noticing it. She gives me little stand-up-straight glances about fifty times a day.)

There was the time I rushed outside just in time to stop Pooch from catching a chipmunk he was about to pounce on. (Okay, it had started raining and I was *really* running out to get a book I'd left in the yard. I just happened to catch the cat at the right time.)

Okay, there was a perfectly ordinary explanation for each of those times—probably. But I couldn't help wondering if there might be a supernatural explanation as well.

Of course I didn't suggest that to anyone. Even the thought of speaking the words *supernatural explanation* out loud made me squirm. I could already hear Jack laughing at me. I kept my thoughts to myself—but I couldn't stop thinking them.

You might have noticed that almost all of these weird coincidences happened inside. That's because I practically didn't get the chance to go outside for five whole days after that storm caught us on the beach. It rained nonstop all that time, and the only exercise Trevor and I got was dashing back and forth from the car on our way to the grocery store.

"Lois Levine was saying it's never been so bad in the whole twenty-five years she's lived here," my mother reported at the dinner table one night. "None of the year-rounders has ever seen so many storms at the beginning of the season."

"Maybe someone let a devil loose on the island," my father said lightly. Dad never cares much about bad weather. Rain means he can take naps without feeling guilty about it. "The weather is certainly mad at us about *something*."

"A devil? Here? What do you mean, Dad?" Trevor looked up nervously from his plate.

My mother shot Dad another one of her looks. This one was her thanks-a-lot look. "Daddy's just kidding, honey," she said in a soothing voice. "Of course there aren't any devils on Moose Island. There aren't any devils *anywhere!*"

Trevor darted a scared glance across the table at me. He didn't say anything more, but I knew what he was thinking.

Vampires aren't supposed to exist, either.

With the weather being so awful, my mother began to run out of fun projects for me and

Trevor. We had already reorganized last summer's shell collection, sculpted clay dinosaurs, made puppets and put on a show, and built miniature buildings out of popsicle sticks. Since she didn't want us sitting around in front of the TV or watching mold grow on the walls, she had to start coming up with not-so-fun projects.

"On your feet, both of you!" Mom hollered one morning after breakfast. She was heading toward the stairs with the vacuum cleaner clumping along behind her. "We're cleaning up the attic today!"

"Oh, *Mom*," Trevor and I groaned in unison. But Mom had yet another look in her eye: the don't-mess-with-me look. There's no point in arguing with her when she gets like that, so we picked up the cleaning stuff she'd put out for us and glumly dragged up the stairs after her.

"Why doesn't *Dad* have to help?" I asked, thumping the banister with the mop I was carrying.

"Dad's fixing the leak in the garage roof," Mom told me briskly. "Of course you're welcome to do that instead, if you'd rather."

"No, thanks," I grumbled, wondering whether my father was going to have any luck fixing a leak during a rainstorm. No one ever said screenwriters had to be practical.

"Anyway"—Mom was trying to sound cheerful—"when the attic's all fixed up, it will make a wonderful playroom for the two of you. I've been meaning to get around to this for *years*."

Trevor slipped his hand into mine as we walked over the attic threshhold. I hadn't been up in the attic for a couple of years, and I had forgotten how dark and gloomy it was. Its one cracked window was so garlanded with spiderwebs that you couldn't see out at all. The drab light from the window revealed piles of old boxes filled with rubbish, toppled stacks of ancient, crumbling books, and broken bits of furniture. A shadowy dressmaker's form, draped with sheets, hovered in one corner like a frozen ghost. There was an old pitchfork propped up against the wall. And over the whole place was a layer of dust as thick as frosting on a cake. Glancing back over my shoulder, I saw that we'd left footprints in it.

"Some playroom, Mom!" I said protestingly. "This is horrible!"

Mom let out a deep breath. "It's a bit worse than I remembered. Let me just find the light switch so we can—"

Her hand fumbled against the wall. We heard a click, and—nothing. The light bulb must have burned out.

"Oh, darn," Mom grumbled, abandoning her

attempt at cheerfulness. "I'll have to run downstairs and get another bulb."

But when she did, the light still didn't work.

"Must be a problem with the wiring," Mom said. "Well, I'll have to run down again and get the flashlights. and a couple of brooms, I guess, since we won't be able to vacuum."

You try cleaning with a flashlight in one hand! "We should strap these lights to our heads, like miners," I told Mom between clenched teeth as I struggled, on tiptoe, to move a box from the top of an old highboy so I could dust under it. "I wonder what's in—"

Suddenly something sank its teeth into my finger.

I cried out and jerked my hand back. In the dim light, I could see a drop of blood on the end of my index finger.

"Mom, there's something alive in that box!" I gasped.

My mother quickly crossed the attic toward me. "Must be a mouse," she said with a grimace. "Yuck!" She lifted the dusty box down from the highboy and squinted into it.

"No," she said in a strangely altered voice. "It's not a mouse. It's a—Meg, it's some kind of animal, but all that's left is its skeleton."

In silence she held out the box so I could see its contents.

24

I wasn't sure I *wanted* to see, but I couldn't keep myself from shining my flashlight into the box.

Yes, that was definitely a skeleton. It was lying curled up on its side, its empty eyesockets staring out vacantly and its wingbones folded into neat V's.

"Is it a bird?" Trevor whispered. He had tiptoed up next to my elbow to look.

"No," said my mother. "Not a bird. Look, it has teeth." She pointed. One of the skeleton's incisor teeth was tipped with blood. "I think it must be some kind of bat," my mother continued.

A *bat!* Shuddering, I pushed the box away. With everything that had happened last summer, a bat was the last animal I wanted to think about.

My mother had brought a big trash can up to the attic. Now she gingerly set the box inside it. "I guess it's not surprising to find something like this up here," she said doubtfully. "After all, bats *do* settle in attics once in a while. And they have to die sometime."

"But—but how could a skeleton bite Meg?" Trevor quavered.

That was exactly the same thing I'd been wondering.

"Oh, of course it couldn't have bitten Meg," Mom assured him. "She just touched one of its teeth when she was reaching into the box." She smiled sympathetically at me. "Though I don't blame you for thinking differently. In a creepy room like this, it's hard *not* to imagine things."

Mom picked up her broom again. "Well, guys, the only way we're going to make this room less creepy is to keep working, isn't it? Once it's all cleaned up and the lights are fixed, you won't believe the difference. So let's get going again!"

And she started sweeping with even more energy than before.

After a second, Trevor started mopping again. But I stood still for a moment, staring down into the bottom of the trash can, where I could barely make out the skeleton's outline.

I knew I hadn't just touched one of its teeth when I reached into the box. I'd been *bitten*, not pricked. I had definitely felt those jaws snap shut on my finger.

"Of course the skeleton couldn't have bitten me," I whispered to myself.

But it had.

I didn't even notice until later, when I was trying to put everything together, that the hand the skeleton had bitten was the one wearing the new ring.

CHAPTER THREE

We never did finish cleaning out the attic. "I guess you're right, Meg," my mother finally admitted after we'd spent about four hours pushing dust from one corner to another. "This *wouldn't* make a very good playroom. Let's get out of here, guys."

I was glad to.

Being bitten by a bat skeleton ought to be proof enough that you've been singled out for some bad luck. I wasn't *asking* for any more proof than that. But over the next few days, I got plenty more anyway.

Thank goodness none of the other bad things that happened were as frightening as the bat skeleton. They were much more ordinary. Ordinary, that is, except for the fact that they all kept happening to *me.*

For instance, on the first nice day after the rain stopped, my family went on a picnic. I was the one who sat on the ants' nest. I was wearing jeans, and about a thousand ants got up my pant legs before I realized what was going on.

The night after that, the headboard on my bed suddenly crashed down on me while I was sleeping.

And the day after that, when Jack and I were sitting out on the dock, *three* waves leaped out of nowhere to splash me. Only me—they left Jack alone. The third wave was so strong it knocked me backwards off the dock into the water.

"Something's out to get me! I swear it!" I sputtered as I climbed back up the steps to the dock.

"It's a pretty low-level something, then," said Jack mildly. "Getting splashed by a wave isn't that rare, you know."

"*Three* waves, Jack. Three waves that didn't even get you damp. And what about the ants' nest? What about the headboard on my bed, and the bat bite?"

"The bat bite I'll let you have," Jack conceded, "if it really happened. The bed and the ants' nest—well, maybe you're just getting clumsy, Meg."

But I hardly heard the insult. I was still digesting the first part of what he'd said.

"*If* it really happened? What do you mean?" I asked indignantly. "I showed you the bite mark on my finger, didn't I?"

"You showed me a mark, yeah. That doesn't mean a skeleton bit you. How could it?"

This was a big change from the way Jack had been last summer. Then he'd been the one who always tried to convince *me* that, say, my babysitter was a vampire and not just a weird teenager. I could still remember the battle I'd had trying to convince him that it wouldn't be a good idea to put a stake through Vincent's heart, just in case he did turn out to be a normal person. I think Jack would much rather have taken the risk.

Now all of a sudden *Jack* seemed to think *I* was the one imagining things! Had the ten months since last summer turned him into a different person after all?

"Okay, Mr. Sensible Grownup," I said as I started wringing ice-cold water out of my T-shirt. "The next time I have a problem, I'll be sure to come to you so you can tell me it didn't happen."

"All I'm saying is you shouldn't jump to conclusions, that's all," said Jack sturdily. "If you—"

Suddenly we heard my mother calling. "Meg? Jack? You have a visitor!"

Startled, we turned around. My mother was heading toward the dock with a girl I'd never seen before.

"Who's that?" I muttered to Jack. I had forgotten that I was mad at him. "Do you know her?"

"Uh-uh. She can't be from around here," Jack muttered back. "I think I would have noticed her before."

The girl, whoever she was, *was* kind of noticeable. She looked about my age, maybe a little older, and she was very, very tan—the kind of industrial-strength tan you get only by working at it eight hours a day. She was wearing a black bikini top and black biking shorts, and she had masses and masses of sun-bleached ringlets. I have to say she had a kind of vacant look on her face, but probably not many people would have noticed her expression.

I wasn't just standing there staring at this girl, of course. You can notice a lot of details about a person in a second or two, which is about how long it took for me to size her up and decide I didn't like her.

Okay, I know that was unfair of me. She hadn't even spoken a word yet. But just let me ask you: wouldn't *you* automatically hate a girl your age who was staring at Jack as though she hadn't had a bite to eat in three days and he was a plate of chocolate-chip cookies? Jack's not my boyfriend or anything, but that doesn't mean I want a lot of other girls drooling all over him!

But suddenly I realized that my own expression might not be that pleasant, either. At least I didn't want my mother to see it. So I quickly pasted on a smile. "Hi," I said as nicely as I could.

"Hi guys," said my mother. "This is—Meg, you're soaking wet!"

I knew my mother wouldn't believe that three waves had just jumped out of the water and attacked me and me alone. "Jack pushed me in," I said. I turned toward Jack and smirked wickedly.

"Hey!" Jack began. He opened his mouth to protest some more, but my mom just laughed.

"You kids!" she said good-naturedly. Then she remembered why she'd come down to the dock. "Meg, Jack, this is Kelly Pitts. She's fourteen. Kelly, this is my daughter, Meg, and her friend Jack Cornell. Jack's family lives down the beach in the other direction."

"Hi, Jack," said Kelly in a breathy voice. She smiled at me without saying anything. Somehow I got the feeling that she considered me to be much, much younger than she was. *Hey, Jack's younger than you are, too!* I wanted to tell her.

"Kelly's parents have just rented that house down the beach from us," Mom continued. "You know, the one with the big weathervane?"

It's actually the closest house to ours, although there's a lot of trees and stuff separating the two places. "Oh, that's a great house," I said enthusiastically. At least I could be nice about Kelly's *house.*

Kelly grimaced. "Yeah, I guess. It's kind of old-fashioned, though."

"Gee," said Jack in an innocent voice. "Around here, most of us *like* old-fashioned houses."

Kelly's expression changed instantly. "Oh, me too! That's what I was about to say—that the *reason* I like it so much is that it's so old-fashioned. There are just so many wonderful . . . uh . . . old-fashioned kinds of Maine-type things in it. You know what I mean?" she finished.

Yes, I knew what she meant.

"Well," said my mother brightly, "I'll leave the three of you to get acquainted. Nice meeting you, Kelly!"

Isn't that *always* the way parents are? They assume that just because someone's the same age as you, you'll be best friends without any problem. When you're little, they tell you to go play. When you're older, they tell you to get acquainted. My mother strolled back to the house and left the three of us to get acquainted.

"What do you guys do for fun around here?" Kelly asked the minute Mom was out of sight.

"Oh, not much," said Jack after a second. "It's kind of dull, really." He faked a yawn.

"Yeah," I agreed, playing along. "Just about all we ever do is go swimming. And the water's freezing."

"Drag city," said Kelly. "I hate cold water."

Then, with a sidelong glance at Jack, she added, "I mean, unless *you* guys would like to swim, of course. See, I'm from North Carolina, and down there the water is a lot warmer than it is here, so I don't really like cold water all that much. But I bet I could get used to it, especially if someone who's used to it, like you guys"—she glanced at Jack again—"showed me the ropes." She paused, took a deep breath, and sailed on. "Because I really, really love to swim, and you know, down in North Carolina where I come from, I swim almost every day, you know? So I bet I could get used to the water here. Besides, if there's some sun I can at least catch some rays, and that's my *really* favorite thing."

Wow. A flirt and a nonstop talker. What a great combination.

Anyway, Kelly rattled on for a few more minutes and then said she had to get back home. "My mother *claims* she needs me to help with some chores around the house. Can you believe it? *Chores!* But I'll see you later, Jack. Oh, and you, too, of course," she added without even using my name.

"Kelly Pitts," said Jack thoughtfully as he watched her walk away. "As in, 'She's the Pitts.' "

"Oh, well," I said forgivingly. I could afford to

34

be gracious now that Kelly was out of sight. "She probably won't bother us again if she has to work on her tan so hard."

Unfortunately, that turned out to be another thing I was wrong about.

"So where's your makeup? Can I look at it?"

It was only a day after we'd met Kelly, and already she was contaminating my room. "I was bored out of my mind at home," she had greeted me a few minutes ago. "I mean, Mom and Daddy keep doing all this stupid unpacking, and we don't have cable and there's nothing for me to do, and when I complained, Mom goes, 'Well, why don't you help for a while?' So I go, 'Yeah, *really*—help take stuff out of *suitcases? That's* a great way to start out a vacation.' Then Mom suddenly gets all crabby, so I decided to get out of there. I mean, can you blame me? So anyway, where *is* your makeup?"

She was standing in front of my bureau, switching back and forth between inspecting her skin in the mirror and snooping around the stuff on top of the bureau. Not that there was much stuff there except for a sandwich bag of ponytail holders and a hairbrush.

"I don't wear that much makeup yet," I confessed. "And not any when we're here." Then I sighed to myself. Somehow Kelly was making me feel like a baby and a prissy old grandmother at the same time. That's why I couldn't ask her to leave my stuff alone. I was afraid it would sound too goody-goody-ish.

"God, I don't know how you can stand going out there with nothing on your face, even if you are only eleven."

"Twelve," I told her.

"Whatever," Kelly said carelessly. She toyed with the knobs on the top drawer of my bureau, then let go when she saw me watching her in the mirror. "I mean, you never know. You might meet some cute guy somewhere—and if you look like a dog, your chances are shot! So anyway, is Jack coming over today?"

"I don't know," I answered. *And I wouldn't tell you if I did know,* I thought. "He might be over after his sailing lesson."

"Wow, sailing! Has he ever taken you for a ride, or a sail, or whatever you call it?"

"Not yet," I said shortly.

"Well, do you mind if I ask him to take me sometime? He's really cute." Kelly giggled, watching me in the mirror again. "You guys aren't going out or anything, are you? I mean, I figure you're too young to go out with anyone." And, before I could say anything, she added, "So you won't mind if he takes me sailing, right?"

Uh, wrong.

Luckily, there was no danger of Jack's taking Kelly sailing. "Unless she can figure out a way to blackmail me into it," he told me privately a couple of days later. Jack wasn't warming up to Kelly any more than I had. In fact, Jack was the one who came up with her new name: Pittsy. Once we'd started calling her that behind her back, it was almost impossible not to slip and say it to her face. At least the suspense of wondering whether we might call her Pittsy by mistake made talking to her more exciting.

Jack was also the one who invented our new game. It was called Dodging Pittsy, and the rules were simple. We had to try never to be anywhere where Pittsy (I mean Kelly) was. Simple, but hard—because Pittsy got into the habit of dropping by at least twice a day.

"I don't understand why you don't like her," my mother said one evening. "She's practically the same age as you!"

Mom was the one who had hired a vampire babysitter the summer before, so I already knew her kid-judgment wasn't too good. Still, if she had heard what Pittsy considered to be conversation, I think Mom would have understood why I wanted to hide in my closet whenever I heard our doorbell ring.

Here is what Kelly liked to talk about: her

looks, how bored she was, her looks, and, once in a while, *my* looks. "You want to catch some rays?" she would ask. "No? Why not? You're so untan you're practically *gray*. . . . Well, you want to send out for pizza? . . . You want to ask your mom if she'll take us to a movie? . . . You want me to streak your hair for you? . . . You want to watch me do a makeover on myself? . . . Hey, do you have Nintendo?"

The minutes would crawl by, and all I would say would be, "No, thanks. No, thanks. No, thanks. Uh, no thanks." At first I wondered why Kelly bothered coming over, since I never wanted to do anything she suggested. But I guess even a measly twelve-year-old like me was more interesting than hanging around at home. And, of course, Jack was more interesting than I was, even though he was getting so good at the game of Dodging Pittsy that he practically never came over to my house anymore.

Well, first we had had terrible weather. Then the world had started ganging up on me. Then Pittsy—uh, Kelly—had moved in next door. Vacation had barely started, but I was wishing it were already over.

Then one day Kelly dropped in with some news. I was reading on my bed (my father had fixed the headboard, of course), and she came in and flung herself down at my desk.

"I met the greatest guy last night!" she told me. "At the Community Center dance, you know?"

The Moose Island Community Center has dances once in a while. Jack and I went to one last year—for vampire-tracking purposes, not to dance—and we had such a terrible time that I've never been to another one.

Kelly was still chattering on. "I think this guy really likes me. And *I* really like *him*. 'Cause you know why?"

"Why?" I asked boredly.

"Well, he's not like all these other babies I've been spending time with. He's really grown-up. And he's a great listener! I feel as though I could tell him anything."

You probably can, I thought. *I bet he never gets the chance to tell you anything, though.*

"Also, he's really sophisticated," Kelly went on. "He's traveled a lot. Even to Europe, you know? And he's really tall and everything."

"Sounds great," I said. I was a little distracted at that point because, for some reason, the ring with the red stone had suddenly started to feel very tight. I tried to pull it off, but it wouldn't *come* off. Finally I resigned myself to the pain and tuned back in to Pittsy.

"Well, it'll sure make things more interesting around here," she was saying.

I hoped it would. Maybe it would make things so interesting that Pittsy wouldn't need to come visit me anymore.

Now, speaking of interesting . . .

All this Kelly/Pittsy stuff didn't change the fact that I kept running into bad luck. (I mean, bad luck besides having Kelly live next door.) As Jack would say, it was all low-level bad luck—there's no reason to bore you with it here. How many times do you need to hear about me falling down the stairs, after all? But it was definitely turning into a routine.

I also kept on being psychic. Once again, it was pretty low-level psychicness, if that's the word I want. I could tell when Pittsy was going to drop by, I knew Trevor was about to spill his cereal, I found Dad's briefcase when no one else could—things like that.

Then, whoever was in charge of all this stuff decided to throw something new into the pot. I started to feel as though someone was watching me.

I'd already been telling myself not to be so paranoid. I was already spending half of every day telling myself that breaking the mirror or guessing that Pooch was about to yawn was the kind of thing that could happen to anybody. So I didn't have a lot of reserves left to tell myself that no one was watching me.

To tell myself that eyes with coal-red pupils were *not* staring into my window at night as I lay there with my heart pounding.

To tell myself that something was *not* breathing over my shoulder when I went down into the basement—and that the something didn't hold its breath when I whipped around to see what it was.

To tell myself that *no* footsteps were following me when I took a walk in the woods, that no one was stopping when I stopped, that my follower was not getting closer, not getting close enough to touch me . . .

To tell myself I was just imagining things. Because, deep down, I was absolutely sure I *wasn't*.

CHAPTER FOUR

"Meg, you and Trevor will be okay if Mom and I stay out after midnight, won't you?" my father asked me anxiously.

"Sure we will, Dad!" I answered with fake heartiness.

"Okay, then. The number's by the phone," Mom chimed in rapidly, checking her lipstick in the mirror. "You can have anything you want to eat from the fridge except the coffeecake—I'm saving it for tomorrow. Trevvie, you go right to bed when Meg tells you. All right, guys. We're off!"

She and my dad kissed Trevor and me and rushed out the door to their car in a jangle of car keys. I turned to my brother.

"Well, Trev," I said cheerfully, "what would you like to do? Shall we make some fudge or play a game or something?"

Trevor looked at me for a second. "You don't have to act like a babysitter, Meg," he said.

"You're my sister. Don't get all polite and have a lot of fun ideas and everything."

"Oh, okay," I said, feeling rather daunted. "Um, do you want to do *anything?*"

"Yup. I want to work on my red-tailed hawk model. In my room. By myself. I'll call you if I need you for anything. You can just go watch TV or something."

He turned and trotted up the stairs, leaving me staring after him. In a second I heard him firmly closing his door.

I guess even little brothers sometimes get older without your realizing it.

Well, I certainly didn't have to waste time whipping up a batch of fudge now—not that I wouldn't have eaten some if there had been some sitting around—so I did as Trevor had suggested. I clicked on the TV and sat down.

Then I realized the phone was about to ring. I rushed over and waited. The first ring had barely even chirped before I picked up the receiver and said, "Hi, Jack."

There was a pause on the other end. "Pretty good," Jack said at last.

I smiled to myself.

"Okay, if you know so much," Jack went on, "what am I going to say next?"

"Sorry. I don't know *that* much."

"I was just going to tell you to tell your parents there's supposed to be another storm tonight. A bad one. Or maybe you knew that already, too."

"No, I didn't. I can't tell my parents anything, either. They just left."

I glanced uneasily out the window. Mom and Dad had left only ten minutes before, at seven thirty. Already it was as dark as midnight outside, and I could hear the surf pounding down on the beach. Pooch was pacing restlessly back and forth around my ankles as though he, too, was upset about something.

"The weather guy on the radio said to get all the lawn furniture and stuff inside," Jack went on.

I guessed that would be up to me.

"The weather guy said it was a bad night for beds falling on people, too." Jack snickered. "Especially girls whose parents are out for the evening."

"Oh, shut up," I said. "You're *so* lame. Well, I'd better go out and bring in the furniture and stuff. Thanks for the warning. Hey," I added hopefully, "want to come over and watch TV?"

"Thanks, but I can't. I promised my dad I'd help him with something. Why don't you ask Pittsy? I bet she's *lots* of fun in a storm."

"Yeah, right. See you."

I hung up, called up to Trevor that I was going

out back for a second, shoved Pooch away from my feet, and dashed out the kitchen door.

The wind was starting up again. For a second, a cloud slid away from the moon and a silvery glow lit up the backyard. All the things that looked so homey and familiar in daylight—our barbecue, the ugly wooden lawn furniture my parents had bought from a catalogue, the pink flamingo someone had given them as a joke— now looked hulking and shadowy.

A branch creaked eerily overhead. Some kind of animal crashed through the woods.

Then a hunched-up figure hobbled awkwardly across the lawn and disappeared under the picnic table.

"What was *that*?" I gasped aloud, leaping back onto the patio. My heart was beating so hard I thought it would choke me.

I clenched my fists and took a deep breath to steady myself. Whatever had run under the picnic table was probably a possum. Or a racoon.

Or some kind of horrible, tiny, hunched-up man waiting with an evil grin to grab my leg when I got close enough . . .

"Meg?" Trevor's frightened little voice floated down to me from his bedroom window. "Are you still out there?"

"Coming right back in, Trev!" I shouted up as

brightly as I could. "I'm just putting some stuff up on the porch!"

Of course it had been a possum. Of course it had.

I set my jaw resolutely, stomped out onto the lawn, and dragged the lawn furniture piece by piece onto the porch. There. Now the storm could do whatever it wanted. And from the sound of it, it wanted to do a lot.

"I'm back inside, Trevor!" I called triumphantly, pulling the kitchen door closed behind me. "I'm going to watch some TV now!" I picked up the cat and plunked myself down on the sofa with him in my lap.

You probably don't care what shows I watched, and even if you did, I'm not sure I'd be able to tell you. Because after a few minutes I stopped paying attention to the television and started paying attention to the weather.

And what clichéd weather it was—right out of a ghost story. There was the *tap-tap-tap* of the branches on the window. There was the frenzied howling of the wind down the chimney, and the sighing of the pine trees it wanted to topple out in the woods. There was the moan of the surf as it broke against the shore. There was the deep, hollow voice whispering my name—

I jumped to my feet so abruptly that Pooch

thudded to the ground and walked crossly away. Hearing my name being whispered was *not* a cliché! *Who was out there?*

"Meg. Meg . . ." The voice sent a crackle of terror through my whole body.

Could it be Trevor? Scaring me didn't seem like something he'd think was fun, but . . . I walked quickly upstairs to make sure he was still in his room.

Not only was my brother still in there, he was asleep in bed. There was a little smile on his face, as though he was having a nice dream, and the half-finished model of a hawk stood guard on his bedside table. He had tucked himself in and turned on his own nightlight without even letting me know.

I closed the door as gently as I could and tiptoed back down the stairs. Whatever was going on downstairs, I had to make sure it didn't wake my brother up.

Could Jack be playing a trick on me? Maybe that was a little more likely, but I could hardly believe he'd go outside on a night like this just to scare me.

"Meg. Meg . . ."

The voice was definitely coming from outside. That meant I'd have to go out into the storm to see who it was.

My hand was shaking as I pulled open the front door and stepped out into the shrieking night.

"Jack?" I called. "Jack, is that you?"

But the wind grabbed my voice away and tossed it into the dark with the rest of the storm noises. Even if Jack had been standing right in front of me, he'd never have heard me in that gale.

And he wasn't standing in front of me. I squinted into the thin, wavering light cast by the lantern on the front porch. No one was there at all.

Something terrible was about to happen. I knew it, suddenly. The storm was closing in—on our house. It was about to swallow me up, and I had only seconds to get away.

I turned sharply and grabbed the door handle again—just as the wind grabbed *me*.

It lifted me into the air as easily as if I were a puff of milkweed. It wrenched at my ankles, then twisted me violently back and forth.

All the time I gripped the door handle as hard as I could. It was like being caught in a riptide—the wind was pulling as hard as the deadliest current. I knew what the wind wanted. It wanted me to let go of the door. It wanted to take me away in its deadly arms—

"No!" I screamed. "You can't have me!" And I kicked backwards as hard as I could.

I had grabbed the door with only my right

48

hand. My left arm was being pulled straight out behind me like seaweed in a current. Now, with all my strength, I brought it up through that fierce current of air, inch by inch.

Halfway there. Every muscle in my body was shaking.

Three quarters of the way. The wind made another desperate try to get my arm back in its control, but I wasn't going to give up now.

The fingertips of my left hand reached the door handle. Slowly, so agonizingly slowly, I pushed my hand forward until it was gripping the handle securely.

Suddenly the wind let go of me—just dropped me like a doll. My feet hit the ground again, and I yanked the door open. I darted inside, slammed it behind me, and locked it.

Then I fell face down onto the rug.

For a few seconds I lay there motionless. I couldn't even think, I was so tired and so relieved. Then I slowly raised my head.

I was safe. I had beaten that terrible storm. And now I could—

"Meg. Meg . . ."

It was only a murmur.

"Meg, I'm back."

I jumped to my feet just in time to see a huge bat fluttering away from the window.

CHAPTER FIVE

"Meg! *Meg!* MEG!"

Cautiously I poked my head out from under the sofa cushion. That didn't sound like the deep, hollow voice that had been terrifying me before. It just sounded like my dad.

"Meg! Honey, are you in there? Open the door!"

Yes, it *was* my dad. I scrambled sheepishly off the sofa and ran to unbolt the front door. I had deadbolted it the instant I had seen the bat.

I had also pushed an armchair and the coffee table in front of the door, covered the windows with blankets, turned off the living-room lights, and hidden under the sofa cushions with the poker from our fireplace clutched in my hand. Then I had lain there, sofa dust tickling my nose, and waited for Vincent Graver to find me.

Because that deep, hollow voice was Vincent's. I knew it was. And the bat outside my window—well, it couldn't have been anyone but Vincent.

I knew that, too. I've had experience in these things.

Vincent was back on the island. And he was looking for me.

If a vampire was looking for you, I'm sure you'd put a few chairs in front of the doors, too. I'm also sure you'd have just as hard a time as I did explaining to your parents why the chairs were there, especially if your parents had tripped over the coffee table the way my parents did.

"Ouch! My shin!" my mother exclaimed as she stumbled through the front door. "What's all this stuff doing here?"

I didn't answer her question. "H-hi, guys," I stammered instead. "You're home early!"

"We got worried about you and Trevor alone in this storm. It's pretty bad out there," my mother said, rubbing her shin where she'd bumped it on the coffee table. Then she got back to her main area of interest. "So anyway, what have you been doing to the living room?"

Now, one thing I learned very early last summer was that there was no way my parents would *ever* believe we were under siege by a vampire. So I didn't even consider telling the truth this time.

"Oh, Trevor and I were just playing—uh—hide-and-seek," I said as offhandedly as I could.

"Hide the poker, you mean?" asked my father dryly. He pointed to the poker, which was sticking out from under the sofa cushions.

"Oh, that was part of a different game. Gosh, I'm tired!" I exclaimed, faking a huge yawn. "I think I'll head right up to bed." And I dashed up the stairs without even waiting for my parents to pay me for babysitting.

"I don't get it," said Jack the next morning. I had called him and asked him to come over right after breakfast, and we were sitting on the dock together, where we wouldn't be overheard. "How can Vincent be back? Vampires have to sleep in the dirt they were buried in, and we threw the dirt from Vincent's coffin into the ocean! There's no way he *could* come back!"

"Not unless the dirt washed up on the beach," I answered in a miserable voice. "That's not totally impossible, is it? After all, remember that black sand we saw on the public beach when I first got here? Maybe—maybe *that* was the dirt from Vincent's coffin."

"Well, maybe," Jack conceded. "But I can hardly believe it."

I could hardly believe it, either. But I knew I hadn't imagined what had happened the previous night.

I shuddered. "If my parents hadn't walked in so early last night, I bet Vincent would have gotten into the house," I said. "Who knows what he might have done?"

"Yeah," said Jack with, I thought, a little too much relish. "Your mom and dad might have found puddles of blood instead of their kids. Or maybe Vincent would have—"

I cut him off quickly. "Well, we've got to stop him before he does anything like that, whatever it is," I said. "We're going to find him, Jack. Today."

"Today?" Jack sounded startled. "But I wanted to go sailing today!"

"You can go another time," I said sternly. "I'm not tracking down any vampires by myself."

"Well, can't you get your dad to help you or something?"

"My *dad?* You think he'd believe me? Besides, Dad's not nearly in as good shape as you are," I added. (Feminine wiles, you know.) "You can fight off Vincent much better than he can."

I'm sorry to report that my feminine wiles had no effect at all.

"It's not that I don't believe you, Meg," Jack said, unconvincingly. "It's just that I—"

"Meg!" my mother suddenly called from the back door. "Kelly Pitts just called. She wants to come over."

54

"Oops! I'm just on my way out, Mom," I yelled back, jumping to my feet. "Tell her I'll see her later, okay?"

I turned to Jack. "I guess I win this round of Dodging Pittsy. I'm not going to be home, so I'm sure she'll track *you* down."

Now Jack was on his feet, too. "On second thought," he said, "I guess I'll come with you. No sense in wasting a beautiful day like this *sailing.*"

As I've already told you, my mother met Vincent when he was working in the blood bank at Moose Island's tiny medical center.

"I bet Vincent's working at the blood bank again," Jack said as we started to bike into town. "Vampires need a *lot* of blood. Where else could he get a constant supply? Let's head over to the blood bank first."

"And do what?" I asked skeptically. "Tell them we're looking for a vampire?"

"Uh-uh. We can tell them we're there to donate blood ourselves. Then we'll have some time to look around while they tap us, or whatever it's called."

"But Jack, I'm not in the *mood* to donate blood today!" I protested. "Why can't we just borrow some white coats and pretend to be technicians or something?"

"Too TV-ish," Jack called back over his shoulder. "This isn't a sitcom, Meg!"

Well, it certainly felt like one when the receptionist at the blood donation room told us we were too young to give blood ourselves. "You have to be eighteen, dear," she said to Jack regretfully.

I wasn't sorry. I know giving blood is a wonderful idea and everything, but ever since Vincent had come into my life I had felt more like hanging onto my blood than giving it away. I didn't like looking at the two people behind the receptionist who were already giving blood. They were lying on cots with tubes in their arms, not even reading magazines—just watching their blood slowly drain into little plastic bags.

"Gee, too bad," I said cheerfully. "Thanks anyway. We'll see you la—"

But Jack interrupted me. "What do you *do* with all that blood, anyway?" he asked.

"Do with it, dear?" The receptionist looked startled. "Why, we use it for patients."

"No, I mean after you unhook the people who give blood. Where do you put the blood that's in those little bags?"

The receptionist's face cleared. "Oh, that goes into the refrigerated storage area down the hall."

"Can we look inside it?" Jack asked politely.

"Oh, I'm afraid not. There's nothing much to see, anyway."

56

"Oh. Well, thanks anyway." As Jack and I walked away he added under his breath, "Thanks for telling us where it is. Because we're still going to check it out."

"Oh, there's nothing much to see," I parroted. "Just a bunch of blood, that's all. Much too boring for—"

" 'Just a bunch of blood' is exactly what Vincent wants," Jack interrupted. "Now, come on, Meg. Your mom used to work here, so I'm sure you can handle it."

Suddenly that gave me an idea.

The door that read Blood Bank did not, I was relieved to see, open into a room filled with blood. Instead it opened into a room occupied by a couple of laboratory technicians. One, a young woman, was inspecting a slide under a microscope and jotting down some notes. The other, a young man, was eating a sandwich. It wasn't exactly a terrifying scene, although the room beyond the technicians—the room that I was sure held the blood—had a metal door that I didn't like the looks of.

"May I help you?" asked the sandwich-eater, putting down the sandwich. Ham and cheese, I noticed.

I glanced quickly down the hall. No, the receptionist wasn't coming after us with the police in tow.

"My mom used to work here," I said. "Mrs. Swain?"

"Sorry," he said. "I don't remember her."

"Oh, that's okay," I answered quickly. "It was just that, uh, she knew someone who worked here who was only a little bit older than we are. His name was Vincent Graver."

The technician who was bent over the microscope—a young woman—unbent and looked up at us. A name label on her white coat read Ms. Ruters. "I remember *him*," she said. "A tall, sort of pale guy, right?"

Jack and I nodded eagerly.

"You know, Vincent just quit one day last summer," Ms. Ruters told us. "He didn't show up—never called to explain or anything, just never came back. Is he a friend of yours?"

"Oh, no!" I said quickly. "Not at all! But he always said that he loved working here, and I was wondering if maybe we could get jobs like his. Volunteer jobs, of course," I added. "I know we're not old enough to really hire."

For a second Ms. Ruters looked at us without saying anything. "What kind of work did you have in mind?" she said at last.

"Well, whatever Vincent did," said Jack. "What *did* Vincent do, by the way?"

"I think he was responsible for seeing that the

blood got put away properly," she answered. "We store it according to blood type, you know. He would take the bags and recheck them to make sure they'd been typed properly, and then put them into the refrigerator."

"Sounds like the perfect job for Vincent," Jack murmured to me.

Ms. Ruters was staring at us perplexedly. "It wasn't that great a job, you know. I don't think you'd have a lot of fun doing it—even if we *could* hire someone your age."

"Could we at least see where he worked?" asked Jack. "We're very interested in all—all aspects of blood technology, you know. We want to be—uh—hematologists someday."

"Well, I guess so," the technician answered reluctantly. "But only for a second. There's not much to see, anyway." She rose to her feet and pulled open the metal refrigerator door. "Come on in."

The room she led us into looked just like the walk-in refrigerator at my school cafeteria, except that instead of being filled with bottles of milk and boxes of apples, the shelves were lined with purplish packets of blood. Ms. Ruters had been right. There wasn't much to see here.

But now she was frowning as he stared around the little room. "Something's wrong here," she said suddenly. "It's all been rearranged." She poked her head back into the front room. "Fred, have you been moving stuff around in here?"

The other technician peered into the refrigerator. "Uh-uh," he said. "Why?"

"Well, look!" said Ms. Ruters. "The bags are all jumbled up! And where's the type O? I don't see *any* O in here!"

Type O blood, my mother had told me, is sometimes called the universal donor. Anyone can be given type O; it's compatible with all blood types.

It would probably be a vampire's first choice, too. Easier to digest, or something.

"Gee," said the sandwich-eater. "None of the surgeons has requisitioned any O recently." Both of them looked worried now. "We'd better check with the receptionist."

They seemed to have forgotten us—or at least they didn't think we'd had anything to do with the problem. Both of them vanished down the hall without even saying a word to us.

"Hey, this is a perfect opportunity for us to gather clues!" Jack whispered.

"Clues? What kind of clues?"

"Fingerprints!" said Jack excitedly. "Fiber samples! Some of Vincent's hair!"

"Are you crazy, Jack? We don't have anything

to check the clues against." I picked up one of the packets of blood. "Even if this was covered with Vincent's fingerprints, how would we—"

Suddenly a huge hand gripped my shoulder.

"May I help you?" came an angry voice from behind me.

For a terrible second I froze. I didn't dare turn around.

That deep, cavernous voice sounded dreadfully familiar.

And what were those warm, wet drops trickling down my neck?

"It's Vincent!" I shrieked.

The grip on my shoulder tightened. Slowly Vincent turned me around to face him.

"Oh, please!" I begged. "Don't bite me! Or anyway, don't bite Jack! I'm the one who dragged him into—"

Then I realized that the person who was turning me around was not Vincent.

It was an orderly. He was carrying an upended mop and a bucket and frowning down at me. As I stared back at him in shock, a few drops of water from the mop spattered onto the floor.

"May I help you?" the orderly asked again.

Now I realized that his voice didn't sound in the *least* like Vincent's. I guess my imagination had been helping out a little.

"We were just looking around," I squeaked. "I like the way the little bags of blood are all in rows like that. C-congratulations! Okay, we'd better be going, Jack!"

I grabbed Jack's arm and yanked him out of the blood bank and down the hall.

"Well, at least you thought about me for once," said Jack with an evil grin as we headed toward the bicycle rack outside the medical center. "Thanks for keeping that guy from biting me, Meg. You're a real pal."

"Oh, shut up," I snapped. I felt as if my face would never be un-red again.

"Where should we go next?" Jack asked. "It's your turn to think of a place."

I tried to force my brain out of the whirlpool of embarrassment it was spinning around in. "What about—" Abruptly I broke off. A picture had just flashed into my head.

It was a vision of the little hunting shack where Vincent had stored his coffin last summer. Jack and I had found the coffin there—and Vincent had found *us* finding it.

"The shack," I said. "Can't we just try the shack? Vincent *could* be back there this year, you know."

Jack paused. "Sure, I'm game. Let's give it a try."

62

We couldn't bike all the way there, because the hunting shack was in the middle of the woods near my house. So we parked our bikes in my front yard and set off through the underbrush on foot.

It was a long trek, and Jack and I both started to get cranky after about ten minutes. "He's not going to be here," Jack informed me. "We're wasting our time. I don't have to be psychic to know *that*."

"Well, then, why did you come along?" I asked angrily, forgetting that he had come because I'd asked him to. "Ouch!" I added. A thorny branch had just gotten tangled in my hair. "You don't have to be here! Go on back and go sailing if you're so—"

Then I stopped. We had reached the clearing where the shack was.

Or where it had been.

There was nothing there now except a patch of charred, blackened ground and a pile of ashes. Smoke was still rising from the ashes. Here and there a still-smoldering ember was glowing red-hot. And the air was filled with the sickening tang of a recent forest fire.

CHAPTER SIX

"I wonder if the shack was struck by lightning," I said in a low voice, staring at the ruined scene before us.

"Yeah," said Jack. He, too, sounded subdued. "All these storms we've been having, I guess. Just one of those things."

He didn't sound as though he really thought it was just one of those things. And I didn't think so, either. It wasn't stormy today. And of all the places in this forest that lightning could strike, why had it picked the exact spot where a vampire had once slept?

I let out a deep breath. "Well, it's getting late, Jack. I should go home for supper. Sorry to ruin your afternoon for nothing."

"It wasn't exactly for nothing," Jack said comfortingly. "At least now we know Vincent isn't here."

"Right. And that means he could be anywhere on the island. He could be watching us now, for all we know."

We walked back through the woods in silence, and *fast*.

Is it any wonder that when I got home I didn't much feel like talking to anyone? And is it any wonder that when my mother told me Pittsy was upstairs *in my room*, I almost exploded?

"Oh, *Mom!*" I wailed in a whisper. "Why did you have to let her in? I don't want to see her!"

"Now, Meg," Mom whispered back. "She said she'd stay only a few minutes. I don't see why you can't be more pleasant to Kelly. I should think you'd be glad to have a nice girl your own age living so nearby."

"She's *not* my own age," I reminded my mother. "And she's not all that nice, either." I gave Mom what I hoped was a withering glance and stomped grumpily upstairs.

"Hi, Pi—uh, Kelly," I said in a flat voice as I walked into my room. "How are—"

"Meg!" Pittsy whooped. She raced over to me and—*yuck!*—threw her arms around my neck. "The greatest thing just happened!" she said shrilly, jumping up and down. "My boyfriend told me he loves me!"

This news was so totally out of the blue that it drove every thought of Vincent from my head. "Why do you think I care?" I snapped, yanking myself out of Pittsy's grip and glaring at her.

Instantly I was sorry, but then I realized that Pittsy hadn't even noticed how mean I'd been. She started jumping up and down and whooping all over again.

"See, I was over at his place this afternoon," she babbled, standing in the middle of the room and making big, theatrical gestures. "And he just, you know, looked into my eyes all of a sudden and said, 'Kelly, I love you,' just like *that!* I mean, I wasn't even expecting it or anything! Isn't that so cool?"

I had walked over to my desk and sat down by that point, my head in my hands. "Kelly, I'm really—"

"And then, you know, he looked into my eyes *again* and said, 'Do you love me?' And I'm like, 'Whoa, this is heavy!' And he looked into my eyes even harder, and—"

"Kelly, maybe you could tell me about this another—"

"So finally I go, 'Yes, of course I do,' and then he *kissed* me!"

Amazingly, Pittsy let out an enormous yawn at that point. Then she perked up again. "So isn't that just so fantastically wonderful?"

"Kelly, it's almost time for—"

"So anyway, I just wanted to tell you about it. And to say that of course I won't be able to spend as much time with you now," Pittsy went on importantly.

That was the first good news I'd heard all day.

"Because after all, I've got to really devote myself to Victor for the rest of the summer."

Victor.

For some reason, that name sent out an alarm. I glanced over at Kelly with sudden interest.

"What did you say his name is?"

"Victor. Victor Grable. Isn't that a great name? It's so—you know—mature."

Victor Grable. Vincent Graver. Same initials. Practically the same name. Could it be—could it, impossibly, be possible—that the person Pittsy was talking about was *Vincent?*

Before I could pursue this thought any further, Pittsy was off and running again. "That's a really neat ring you're wearing, Meg. Where'd you get it?"

"My ring?" Startled, I followed her gaze to the strange ring on my hand. Its dark red stone glinted dully up at me. "Gee, I'd almost forgotten I had this! It was in the bottom of our washing machine, for some reason."

"You'd almost forgotten you had it?" said Pittsy eagerly. "So you don't like it that much, that means. Can I have it, then? It would look really great with my—with my jeans."

I was still thinking so hard about the Victor/Vincent thing that I almost told her, "Sure." But then a second alarm went off in my head, and I looked up at Pittsy's face again.

It was much more—I don't know—more sharp and cunning than I'd ever seen it before. Usually Pittsy didn't have much expression at all. Now, though, she was watching me from under her eyelids in a very furtive way. And suddenly I was on my guard.

As I stared at her face I noticed something else. Didn't Pittsy look paler than usual, especially for someone who worked on her tan as much as she did? And her eyes . . . wasn't she more hollow-eyed, somehow? More—more *vampire-y*?

I closed the hand with the ring on it into a fist. "Oh, I don't much feel like giving it away, I guess," I said as casually as I could.

"Why not? I don't see why not!" Pittsy's voice had sharpened. She took a step toward me. "I really like that ring! I would think you could do me just this one favor, Meg. Since I'm always so nice to you."

So nice to me? My jaw dropped. I couldn't think of anything to say.

"So you're not going to give the ring to me?" Pittsy asked crossly.

"Um, well, no. I—I'm sorry." Why was my

voice faltering? After all, I didn't *owe* Pittsy the ring!

"Okay, then, I guess there's no point in my staying. Thanks a *lot*, Meg," said Pittsy sarcastically. "You're a really great friend."

And she flounced out of my room in a snit.

A couple of minutes after that, my father called up to tell me that supper was ready. In a daze I walked downstairs, in a daze sat down at my place, in a daze started to eat.

What was going on?

Was Pittsy really going out with Vincent? And if she was, was he turning her into a vampire? And where did the ring fit in, anyway?

"Meg, you're hardly eating." My mother's voice broke into my thoughts. "I thought spaghetti and garlic bread were your favorites!"

I looked down at my plate. Mom was right—spaghetti and garlic bread *are* my favorites. I'd been thinking so hard I hadn't even noticed what we were having. (And for that to happen, I *have* to be thinking hard.)

"Sorry, Mom. I've got a lot on my mind, I guess. Trevor, would you please pass the garlic bread?"

"Sure," answered my brother. He shoved the basket of bread in my general direction and continued chattering away to my father. "So, Dad, the parent seagulls have this red spot under their beaks, and when the babies see it, that's their signal to open *their* beaks to be fed. Isn't that neat, Dad? And if you put lipstick on your thumb and hold it over a baby seagull's face, it will open its beak for you! Can we try it sometime, Dad?"

"Sure, if we can find a baby seagull," my father answered.

"And Dad, then could we take it home and raise it? A seagull would be a good pet, don't you think?"

"Well, Trevor, we'd have to see about that," said my dad cautiously. "You see, a gull is a . . ."

At that point, I tuned out again. For some reason, Trev's mentioning a red spot had made me think of blood. And that made me think of Vincent again. And *that* got me started wondering about Pittsy again. When supper was over, I could hardly believe I'd eaten five pieces of garlic bread without even noticing.

My thoughts were whirling around so uselessly that after supper I decided to take a walk on the beach. The house seemed too crowded with everyone else in it. I couldn't concentrate with Trevor running around looking for something to do and Dad trying to get us to dry the dishes and Mom suddenly threatening to make me and Trevor pose for Christmas-card pictures "since we're all so relaxed and cozy," she said. So I escaped.

It's beautifully strange out on the beach at night. Even when there's no moon—and there wasn't one that night—the ocean still glimmers faintly, and you can almost imagine it's lighting your way. All along the beach you can see the faraway lights of houses looking cozy and remote at the same time. The night breeze blows just enough to make you wish you'd brought a sweater but not enough to make you actually want to go get one. It's kind of a poetic time to be out, if you know what I mean.

As long as no one's following you, that is.

When I'd been out on the rapidly darkening beach for no more than five minutes, I heard footsteps walking lightly behind me. Sometimes other people walk along the beach at night, so I didn't pay any attention at first. But then whoever it was didn't pass me as I'd been expecting. As he or she got closer, the steps became slower.

Was someone trying to catch up with me? I turned around to see, but it was too dark to see anything now.

"Anyone out there?" My voice sounded faint and trembly in the dark.

No answer. I turned and headed toward the light I knew was my house.

I didn't dare run. Somehow it seemed as though once I started running, whoever was behind me would *definitely* start chasing me. Instead I walked faster, and then faster still. The thought passed fleetingly through my head that I must look as stupid as those race-walkers I sometimes see striding through my neighborhood at home. But I didn't care. As long as I didn't show how afraid I was, the person behind me might not hurt me.

Suddenly someone grabbed the back of my T-shirt and pulled me to the ground.

I tried to scream, but my pursuer was pressing my face into the sand. I kicked as hard as I could, but my feet just flailed against the empty air. A whimper of terror escaped my throat. Was I going to die right here?

Then a hand reached for mine. It closed around the ring I was wearing—the ring Pittsy had wanted. And it began to tug.

It had to be Pittsy, I thought. She just couldn't believe I wasn't going to let her have her way. So instead she'd decided to bully me into giving in.

Well, she wasn't going to get away with it! With all my strength, I flung myself up onto my knees. I wrenched my hand away from my attacker—Pittsy, I was sure—and slammed a fist into her stomach.

I heard a grunt of fury from the shadowy figure in the dark. And then two sharp-nailed hands grabbed me around the throat, pulling me closer and closer. . . .

I screamed a big, garlic-breath scream.

There was a gasp of disgust from my attacker.

I screamed again, louder and more garlicky this time.

My attacker let go of me and raced off down the beach.

I ran home myself, of course. Just before I reached the back door, I stopped short and reached out a hand to steady myself against the house while I got my breath back. I had to go in looking as normal as I could.

Why? Because Mom and Dad might not believe me—and it wouldn't really help if they did. They might call the police, but what could the police do? There was no proof that anything had happened. Besides, poor Trevor would be so frightened that he'd never want to go to the beach again.

No, it definitely wasn't worth it. So I just leaned against the house and panted until I could breathe normally.

All this fuss about a ring . . .

I glanced down at my hand. In the light flowing

out from the kitchen, the ring's red stone was clearly visible.

I bit back a scream of terror as I stared at it.

A face was glaring murderously up at me from the center of the stone. It was a face so deathly pale, so cadaverously thin, with such burning dark eyes, that I recognized it right away.

"This is Vincent's ring!" I gasped.

CHAPTER SEVEN

I should be an actress when I grow up.

"Hi, hon," said my mother as I walked into the kitchen. She, Dad, and Trevor were reading peacefully at the kitchen table. "Have a nice walk?"

"Yes, it was great," I said. I couldn't hold back a shudder, but I managed to turn even that into part of my act. "Brrrr! It's kind of cold out there, though. I think I'll go take a hot shower and get ready for bed."

"Gosh, you're going to sleep even earlier than I am," observed Trevor with satisfaction.

"Oh, I'm not going to sleep." *That* was for sure. I was feeling so jumpy that I couldn't believe I'd ever fall asleep again. "I've got to call Jack after I shower."

"Well, good night, honey," said my father, "and don't talk too late. Whatever you have to say will keep until tomorrow."

No, it wouldn't.

Mom blew me a kiss.

Trevor returned to his bird book.

"Good night, Meggo," said my father.

" 'Night!" I said as brightly as I could. And I headed upstairs at a run.

Our hall phone has a nice long cord—long enough to let me bring the phone into my bedroom and close the door. So that's what I did once I dialed Jack's number.

"Meg! Hi! Listen, I gotta call you back later," Jack said when he answered the phone. "I'm watching this really great movie. The guy's about to be swallowed by a—"

"No, I have to talk to you right now," I interrupted. "Believe me, no movie you're watching could possibly be as exciting as what just happened to me."

And I told him what *had* just happened to me.

"Yeah," said Jack doubtfully when I'd finished.

" *'Yeah'*? That's all you have to say?"

"Yeah. I mean, I'm sorry you had a scare and everything, but is there any way to prove who attacked you?"

"Vincent! Who else?"

"Well, it could have been Pittsy. She wants the ring, too, you said. Did you get any real clues as to your attacker's identity?"

" 'As to my attacker's identity'? You've been reading too many detective books."

77

"Stop repeating everything I say," Jack said irritably. "I'm just trying to help."

"Okay, okay," I apologized. "Sorry. Anyway, whoever grabbed me had long, sharp fingernails. They really dug into my neck." My skin crawled at the memory. "Vincent's got pointed fingernails, you know," I added. "I noticed them last summer."

"So does Pittsy, though," Jack reminded me. "Haven't you ever noticed hers? She's got one of those death-grip manicures. It makes her hands look about five hundred years old."

"Okay. So that doesn't solve anything," I agreed. "Well, whoever grabbed me on the beach went for my ring first. It makes sense that Vincent would try to get his own ring back, doesn't it?"

"I guess so," Jack said doubtfully. "But maybe Pittsy wants the ring so badly she was even willing to attack you to get it. Or maybe it was just some murderer hanging around the beach." He chuckled, but I tried to ignore it.

"Then there's the garlic," I went on. "I ate a lot of garlic bread at supper."

"I'm glad we're talking on the phone instead of in person, then. But what does garlic have to do with anything?"

"Well, vampires hate garlic. Remember? And

whoever grabbed me let go when I screamed." I blew a sample breath up toward my nose, just to test what I smelled like now. *Gee,* I thought, *brushing your teeth doesn't really get rid of the smell of garlic, does it?*

"Okay, that's a good point," Jack said. "On the other hand, maybe you reeked so badly that *anyone* would have dropped you and run. It's not that I don't believe you, exactly," he added. "I just don't want us to go off on another wild-vampire chase like the other day."

Through the wall I could hear Trevor walk into his room and start getting ready for bed. I knew Mom and Dad would make me get off the phone soon, so I moved on to the next question.

"Well, assuming that this *is* Vincent's ring, how did it turn up in our washing machine?"

"That's a toughie," said Jack. He was starting to sound a little bored, I realized. "I guess he must have done some laundry at your house."

"Never. I'm sure of that." I bit my lip, thinking. "I wonder . . . could the ring have fallen off his hand sometime—when he was babysitting here, I mean—and rolled into the washing machine?"

"Uh-huh. Good idea." Now I was sure Jack was watching his movie again.

"Well, no, it's not, really," I mused. "Because if that had happened, why didn't we discover the ring last summer? After all, we spent the whole second half of the summer without Vincent, and my parents did about nine million loads of laundry after you and I got rid of him."

"Uh-huh," said Jack again.

"Wait a minute, Jack. The bag! That's it, the bag!"

"No. You wait a minute," said Jack. "What bag?"

"The bag of laundry! Of course! You know, on the first day we got here this summer I found this old canvas bag full of mildewy old sheets and things. I didn't tell you about it, I guess."

"Gee, I don't know why not," said Jack innocently.

"Oh, shut up. Anyway, it was the same canvas bag you and I used to carry that dirt we stole from Vincent's coffin!"

"Really?" Suddenly Jack sounded as though he was paying more attention. "Are you sure?"

"Absolutely. We have only one big canvas bag like that. I threw it in the washing machine the second I found it. And a couple of hours after that, Mom brought the ring in to me and said she'd just found it in the washing machine."

"But we dumped all the dirt that was in the bag into the ocean!" Jack protested. "Why didn't the ring fall out, too?"

"Well, it's kind of spiky. It must have caught

on the inside of the bag somehow, on one of the seams or something. It must have stayed in the bag when we dumped out the dirt. And we must have brought it home with us. And . . . and that's what must be going on.

"You know," I continued, "if the ring *is* Vincent's, that would explain a lot. It would explain why I've been sort of psychic on and off ever since I got the ring. And why all those weird accidents keep happening to me. I mean, maybe there's a curse on the ring if someone wears it who's not supposed to!"

"But where do you fit Pittsy into all this?" asked Jack.

"I bet Vincent asked her to get the ring for him."

"*If* this Victor Grable really is Vincent Graver," Jack pointed out. "We're still going to have to prove that, somehow."

"I know it sounds weird," I said desperately. "But I also know I'm right. Don't ask me how I know. I just do."

Abruptly, as if someone had flipped a switch somewhere, my finger with the ring on it began to throb.

"I *must* be right," I said, almost in a whisper. "The ring is sending me some kind of signal."

"A signal? What kind of—"

All of a sudden my dad peeked into my room. "It's getting late, Meg," he said kindly. "Cut this call short, okay?"

"Okay, Dad. Just a few more seconds, I promise."

"What kind of signal? What kind of signal?" Jack was repeating when I turned back to the phone.

"Like a shock, sort of. As if the ring is sending out these pulses of electricity."

"No! No!" Jack howled. "Don't add something *else* to this story! An electric vampire ring that belongs to a vampire we still don't know for sure really exists, and maybe he's going out with a girl except she says her boyfriend has a different name? Listen, Meg, this is getting a teeny bit too weird. Are you still wearing the ring?"

"Yes. I was afraid to take it off," I confessed. "I'm worried about what might happen if Vincent gets it."

"Well, hang onto it. I want us to pin down that ring's powers before we do anything else," said Jack. "And if it turns out not to have any powers—well, then I won't take the call the next time you phone me during a movie."

Luckily, my mother and father were due to go out the next night, and I was going to be sitting for Trevor again. All I had to do was ask if Jack could come help me babysit. My parents said that would be okay, and that they'd give him a ride back to his house when they got home. ("You're not old enough for us to worry about your having boys over," Mom said. She didn't realize she was insulting me, but I let it pass.)

Then, once my parents left, all I had to do was wait for Trevor to fall asleep. Since he had gotten up at four in the morning to go on some Community Center birdwalk, that wasn't hard. I tucked him in and tiptoed down the stairs to Jack, who was flipping through a magazine in the living room.

"All ready for the ring seance?" he asked.

"I—I guess so," I said. With Jack actually sitting in my house, my story was starting to seem thin. I halfway wished I hadn't told him about the ring at all.

"And what exactly are you planning to *do* with the ring?" said Jack.

"I don't know," I admitted. "I thought I would recite that spell we read about last year—you know, the one that's supposed to raise vampires from the dead?" (Last summer we did a lot of vampire research at the library, and one of the things we turned up was an old magic spell that people sometimes used to call forth vampires.) "And—well, we could just see what happens."

"That's *all*? You got me over here to watch you recite a *spell*?"

"It'll take only a second," I said weakly. "Unless you have a better idea. . . ."

I cleared my throat and began to speak. *"I conjure and command thee, spirit of the deceased, to answer my demands."*

Jack and I stared earnestly at the ring, but nothing happened. I fixed my gaze on the stone and continued.

"Berald, Balbin, Gab, Gabor, Arise, Arise, I charge and command thee."

Silence.

A coal fell apart in the fireplace.

More silence.

"Well, this isn't exactly convincing me," said Jack after a second. "Maybe we should think of something else."

"Let me try it again," I said. "Maybe I didn't say it with enough expression before. *I conjure and command thee, spirit of the deceased, to answer my demands. Berald, Balbin, Gab, Gabor, Arise, Arise, I charge and command thee."*

I shivered involuntarily. Hundreds and hundreds of years had passed since the spell had first been spoken. But the strange words still hadn't lost their power.

Except that they didn't seem to be accomplishing much right now.

"Oops," I said. "I'll try it just one more time."

"No, don't bother." Jack stood up and stretched. "I might as well go home," he said. "I don't think this ring has anything to do with Vincent. It's probably just a piece of old junk, as far as I'm—"

Zzzzzzap!

A bolt of lighting leaped out of my ring and darted ten feet across the room. It left behind it a puff of smoke and a suffocatingly evil smell.

Then the dark red stone in the middle of the ring began to glow like fire.

"Jack, look!" I gasped, and he dashed over to stand next to me.

Brighter and brighter the stone burned. And then, in the center of that fiery glow, the image of Vincent's furious face appeared.

"Meg . . ." Vincent growled. *"You cannot escape me this time."*

Up in his bedroom, Trevor suddenly screamed.

CHAPTER EIGHT

When I pushed his door open, Trevor was sitting bolt upright in bed. As the light from the hallway streamed into his room, I could see that his face was almost unrecognizable with terror.

"Meg! Meg!" he sobbed, reaching his arms out to me like someone much younger than seven.

"What is it, Boo-boo?" I dropped down onto his bed and hugged him. "Does something hurt?"

"Vincent was here! He was trying to get me!" cried Trevor.

My heart actually skipped a beat. It did. I could feel it. "No, no, honey," I said soothingly. "You were having a bad dream, that's all."

Trevor shook his head emphatically. "No, I wasn't! I was asleep, and he woke me up! He's right there, outside my window! He was trying to come in!"

"Oh, of *course* he's not out there," I said. "Look, I'll go and see for you." Heart pounding, I walked over to the window.

There was a thin curve of moon behind a pine tree, and a few scattered stars in the black sky. I could see the sloping shadow of the garage, and Pooch walking lazily toward the house. If I hadn't just seen Vincent's face myself, I would have thought it all looked very peaceful.

But I didn't have to tell Trevor anything about my own fears. "He's *definitely* not out there, Trev," I said, forcing out a reassuring laugh. "No one's outside but Pooch—and I should go down and let him in now. It was just a dream. I know it seemed real to you, but how could it have been? Vincent went away a long, long time ago."

I didn't convince myself, but I did a good job with Trevor. (Further proof that I should be an actress when I grow up.) When he was all settled again, I went back downstairs.

Jack was staring at the fire as I walked into the living room, but he turned around to face me.

"I'm really sorry, Meg," he said, and I could tell by his expression that he was. "Vincent *is* back. I should have known you weren't the kind of person to make up something like this. Go ahead and make fun of me. I deserve it."

"I wouldn't *dream* of making fun of you," I said with a saintly smile. "I'd *much* rather drive you crazy being all syrupy and forgiving. Like this. How do you like it so far?"

Jack grimaced wryly. "I guess I'll have to get used to it. Listen, I know your parents said they'd drive me back, but it's late and I've got to go home. I promise I'll be over first thing tomorrow morning so we can work out some kind of strategy."

The next morning, on my last bite of breakfast, Jack walked through the front door. When I'd finished, we headed up to my room to talk. (My parents were working in the yard, and Trevor was trying to tame a robin without much success.) "Have you had any more trouble with the ring?" he asked respectfully once we were upstairs.

I glanced down at the dark red stone. "Not yet," I said. "It's been—" Then I stopped in dismay. "Oh, no. Someone's here!"

"What? I don't hear anyone," Jack said—and then we both heard the front door open. A second afterward, feet started up the stairs. Not just feet, I mean—a whole person. "Meg?" someone called breathlessly. "Are you up here?"

I smacked my forehead in disgust and silently mouthed "Pittsy" to Jack. "In my room," I answered reluctantly.

"Oh, fantastic!" And in a second Pittsy, too, was in my room.

"Hi, guys," she said, still in the same breathless voice. "Gee, am I tired. I ran all the way here! I think I strained my leg muscles."

Pittsy really did look kind of terrible. She was even paler than she had been the day before, with a strange grayish cast under her fading tan. Her hair was dull and frayed-looking, and there were huge shadows under her eyes.

"Why were you in such a hurry?" I asked warily.

"Because I—" Pittsy began. Then she winced a little and pointed at my window. "Could you pull down the shade first? That stupid sunlight is really hurting my eyes."

Startled, I got up to pull the shade as Pittsy rattled on. "Anyway, I wanted to get here because I wanted so badly to apologize. *How* could I have been so rude to you yesterday? When you're such a good friend to me and all?"

"Well, that's a change," I blurted out without thinking. "I mean, that's all right," I corrected myself lamely. "Everyone has bad days—"

"Because our friendship is much more important to me than a stupid old ring!" Pittsy interrupted again. "I hope you believe I'm telling the truth."

I might have believed it, except that as Pittsy spoke her eyes slid greedily to my hand. And once she saw the ring, she couldn't stop staring at it. She reminded me of Pooch when we open a can of tuna that he knows we're not going to share with him. He just sits at our feet drooling.

"So I just wanted to tell you that I really don't . . . want . . . the ring . . . after all," Pittsy continued reluctantly, with a yearning look at my hand. "Please just forget everything I said yesterday."

"I didn't see you on the beach last night, did I?" I asked abruptly. I hoped I could trick her into confessing by changing the subject fast.

Pittsy's eyes widened. "On the b-beach?" she stammered. "At night? Why would I be out there?"

"I don't know," I answered innocently. "I was just wondering."

"Well, you can stop wondering," Pittsy said sharply, "because I wasn't there when you saw me. I mean, whoever you saw there wasn't me."

Then, unexpectedly, she whirled around and frowned at the window. "That stupid sun, glaring like that!" she snapped. "I feel as though it's trying to *get* me! You must have cheap window shades or something."

I glanced over at Jack and saw that he was as startled as I was. Maybe you could see a teeny bit of sun around the edge of the window shade, but that was it. The room was certainly too dark for *me*. And anyway, why was Pittsy criticizing the sun when she'd been such a total sun-worshiper before?

And weren't her teeth pointier than I'd remembered them? I don't spend a lot of time gazing into people's mouths, but you do notice it when someone's *front* teeth look pointed.

And when she finally told me and Jack she had to leave ("Victor must be *crazy* wondering where I am!"), why did she stare so hard at Jack's neck on the way out?

"Are you thinking what I'm thinking?" said Jack slowly, when the sound of Pittsy's footsteps had died away.

"If you're thinking that she's acting like a vampire, then yes, I am."

"It's hard to miss," said Jack. "I thought she was getting ready to bite me goodbye. Vincent must be turning her into a vampire, too!"

"This is terrible," I said. I was actually wringing my hands. "We haven't even found Vincent yet, and now . . . what's the rule about turning people into vampires? Does it happen the first time a vampire bites someone?"

"Uh-uh," said Jack. "I think it has to be three times. Maybe she hasn't been transformed all the way yet. We might still be able to save her." Suddenly Jack jumped up from his chair with such vigor that he knocked it over. "We've got to track

Vincent down, Meg," he exclaimed. "We have to stop him. And we have to do it today!" Then Jack's face fell. "Only I can't. I've got a sailing lesson in about half an hour. I guess we'll have to wait until tomorrow."

"No, we won't," I declared. "*I'll* track Vincent down on my own. I can do it, Jack. I know I can. I—I bet the ring will help me do it."

If I can just figure out how to ask it politely, I added to myself.

But before I even started thinking about where to look for Vincent, I knew I would need some garlic. And not garlic bread, either. Straight garlic. In cloves. I wanted it as powerful as I could get it.

Cloves of garlic are hard to carry, though—especially when you're running away from a murderous vampire. (I've had experience with this.) So I decided to buy one of those big long garlic braids at a gourmet store downtown called the Buttery.

Every corner of the Buttery has something you want, even if you're only a kid who isn't going to have her own kitchen for fifteen or twenty years. I love going in there just because of the way it smells. There are trays loaded with big gooey caramel brownies and racks filled with millions of spices and baskets heaped with tiny white cheeses on grape leaves. Even the paper napkins are so pretty that I used to use them for craft projects when I was little.

Unfortunately, the one time you *don't* want to go to the Buttery is right before lunch. That's when everyone starts streaming in and saying, "Oh, and why don't you give me half a pound of the wild-rice salad while you're at it," and you have to wait in line behind someone who wants a whole ham sliced extra thin. Also, the Buttery has a restaurant, and anyone who isn't buying take-out stuff for lunch seems to eat in the restaurant instead. So it took much longer than I'd expected before I walked out of the store with three braids of garlic around my neck and no money left in my pocket. (The Buttery is not exactly cheap.)

To my amazement, my parents were crossing the street toward the Buttery just as I walked out. "Hi, Meggie!" my mother called happily. "What are you doing here?" Luckily she didn't wait for an answer. "Daddy and I are playing hooky! We got so tired of working that we decided to go out for lunch."

"Vould you like to join us, mademoiselle?" my father asked in a fake French accent that would have embarrassed me right through the sidewalk if I hadn't had so much on my mind.

94

"No, thanks, I guess," I said. "Where's Trevor?"

"Oh, he's at home," Mom told me. "Kelly Pitts is looking after him. In fact, that's what gave me and Daddy the idea to go out for lunch. Kelly came over to see if she could help us with anything, and we put her to work babysitting your brother."

"*What?*" I shrieked. The ring throbbed warningly on my finger. "She's *alone* with Trevor?"

"She sure is. Wasn't that nice of her?" asked Mom. "You know, Meg, you really should give Kelly another chance. I'm sure she'd be a good friend once you got to know her, and—"

"Hey, you're right!" I broke in. "In fact, I'll go home and make friends with her right now! Thanks for the idea!"

I jumped onto my bike and pedaled furiously away, leaving Mom and Dad on the sidewalk staring after me.

But it turned out that there was no need to hurry. When I got home, the house was empty.

Trevor had disappeared.

CHAPTER NINE

As the police would say, there was no sign of a struggle. No trail of blood led out the door. No furniture had been knocked over. No scuff marks marred the floor from someone being dragged across it. No windows were broken. And Trevor's denim jacket wasn't hanging on its hook—which meant he had probably put the jacket on before he left. Which meant, in turn, that at least he hadn't been dragged out of the house. So there was probably nothing for me to worry about.

But Vincent's ring was feverishly pulsing on my hand, and I *was* worried. If everything had been okay—if there had been a perfectly innocent reason for Pittsy's taking Trevor away—wouldn't she have left a note?

"Trevor! *Trevor!*" I shouted, my voice sounding thin and quavery in the empty house. I knew it would be no use. The only living thing I could see from where I stood was Pooch. He was staring wide-eyed at me from under a chair in the living room.

"Where's Trevor, Pooch?" I couldn't help asking it aloud. Whatever had happened to my brother, Pooch had watched it—and now he was watching *me* as though to see what was going to happen next.

Well, I didn't have any idea what was going to happen next. Had Pittsy kidnapped Trevor? Was this the kind of thing I was supposed to call my parents about? No, they'd just think I was making a fuss about nothing. "She's probably taking him for a walk," I could imagine my mother saying. "Honestly, Meg. You shouldn't be so suspicious!"

Okay, then. Maybe Pittsy *was* taking Trevor for a walk. That was the least nerve-wracking thing to think, anyway. Maybe I could even do something radical, like going over to Pittsy's house and seeing if she and Trevor were there. I grabbed a sweater—the sky was looking ominous again, for the second time that day—and scribbled a quick note to my parents telling them not to worry. (There was no sense in frightening them before I absolutely had to.) Then I dashed for the front door.

A long, long time ago, or so it seemed, I had told Pittsy how much I liked her family's house. (It's right on the water, and it's really old.) That had been the first and last time I had thought about her family. So when I rang the front door-bell and Mrs. Pitts answered the door, I almost burst out laughing despite my fears. Not only did she look exactly like a grown-up, worn-out Pittsy—leggings and everything—but her lips were all bound up around the edges with some kind of weird green tape.

"May I help you?" Mrs. Pitts mumbled stiffly through the tape.

"I'm Meg Swain," I said. Then, before I could stop myself, I blurted out, "What's that stuff on your mouth?"

"Anti-wrinkle treatment."

It didn't sound as clear as that, of course, because of the tape. It sounded more like, "Ah-ee inkle tee-ent."

"I see," I said, feeling like an interpreter. "Um, I was wondering if Pi—uh, Kelly was here."

"Ah you a feh uh Keh-ee's?"

"Feh" was probably "friend." I dodged that question. "We live next door to you. She's babysitting my little brother. Do you have any idea where they went?"

"Ey muh ha tay-en a alk own uh ee."

"Excuse me?"

"They muh ha tay-en a oo-alk down the each," Mrs. Pitts said more clearly.

"Oh, a walk down the beach? Did you see which direction they went?"

"Uh-uh. Sah-y."

"Oh, that's okay," I said forlornly.

If a kid had come to the door and asked *my* mother questions like these, Mom would have tried to find out if something was the matter. But I could see that Mrs. Pitts had already put me out of her mind. She was giving her lips little experimental pats now. "I ha a go," she said, glancing at her watch. "Ti a tay uh tay aw."

"Oh, time to take the tape off?" I was starting to get the hang of Pitts-language. "Well, thank you."

"Ooh eh-kuh," Mrs. Pitts sang out. "Eye-eye."

Whew! I shook my head as I walked away. My own mother sometimes drives me crazy, but I don't think she would ever wear lip tape.

As I walked away from the house, though, my sense of humor evaporated quickly. Now where was I going to look? "A walk down the beach" could be anywhere. There's beach running all the way around the edge of Moose Island. I would probably find Pittsy and Trevor if I walked around the whole perimeter, but it might take too long. . . .

I stopped and gave myself a mental shake. What would Jack suggest if he were here? I stared out at the ocean and tried to imagine—and suddenly I could hear Jack's voice as plainly as if he were speaking right into my ear.

"I thought that ring you found was supposed to be supernatural," he would have said, half teasing and half serious. "Why don't you ask *it* where your brother is?"

The ring! *Thanks, Jack,* I wanted to say. Any ring that gives you second sight should at least be able to help you find your brother!

I walked across the beach to my parents' dock, sat down, and stared intently into the murky depths of the dark red stone.

"Oh, ring," I whispered. I was so worried that I didn't even feel stupid talking to a piece of jewelry. "I know you probably hate me to be wearing you. But can't you help me out this once? Won't you tell me where Trevor is?"

The cold red stone seemed to brighten a little as I stared at it. Then it was still again.

"Please," I said. "I—I'll get you back to Vincent. I promise. Just do me this one favor, okay?"

The ring pulsed a second time, more strongly now. The red stone's surface began to dimple and churn, as though it were somehow liquifying. And then, as I watched, a tiny picture floated up into the stone's center, like a vision in a crystal ball.

"Thank you," I breathed.

One after another, miniature pictures swam across the stone. They couldn't have been more than half an inch high, and yet they were so clear and bright that I could make them out perfectly. First I saw waves dashing against a huge pile of jutting, jagged rocks. Then, a lighthouse silhouetted against a deserted stretch of beach.

And then the stone showed me my brother's face. He was shouting angrily at someone I couldn't see. But he also looked as though he was about to burst into tears.

The stone began to bubble again. The pictures vanished, and I was left staring stupidly at a blank ring.

I jumped to my feet in dismay. "Is that *all*?" I wailed. "That's not fair!"

No, it wasn't all. Because as I stood there, I realized that the ring was telling me where to go. All I had to do was listen to it.

"How can you listen to it when it's not making any noise?" Jack would have said, sensibly, at that point. And at that point I wouldn't have known exactly how to answer. Well, a bird wouldn't know how to explain why it migrates, either. All I knew was that the ring had turned my hand into some kind of compass for my body to follow. And I followed it.

The ring guided me back off my dock, down the beach past Jack's house, and past the three houses on the other side of Jack's. A few people sunning themselves on the sand waved as I passed by, but I didn't wave back. I was too busy concentrating on my directions.

Now the beach was becoming rockier, and the ring had taken me past the section with houses on it. It was much harder to walk here. Rocks kept wobbling treacherously under my feet. Once I slipped and pitched forward, wrenching my ankle so hard that I yelped in pain. But somehow I scrambled to my feet and kept on going.

The groves of pine trees lining the beach were thicker here. The trees watched in solemn silence as I lurched along. A bunch of crows wheeled overhead, making their usual raucous laughter.

"Where *am* I?" I muttered to myself as the crows shrieked their insults at me. "What part of the island *is* this? I never even knew it was here!"

As the beach turned rockier the air became mistier. Soon great draping swaths of fog had cut me off from everything familiar. I turned to look behind me, and saw nothing but fog. I squinted into the fog ahead of me.

There, looming out of the mists, was the group of jagged, treacherous boulders I had seen in the ring's red stone. They were right on the water's edge. Huge, dark green waves were curling and hissing and frothing around them, and as I came closer I could see a bedraggled seagull trying to land on one of the boulders. The wind kept beating it back until it finally gave up and flew away.

Head down, I scuttled by the rocks as quickly as I could. When I raised my head again, I saw the lighthouse I had seen in the ring.

It was towering sternly against the sky, but when I looked more closely I could see that it was old and crumbling and weather-beaten. The lamp room at the top was empty. Except for a small barred window under the lamp room and a heavy wooden door at the bottom, the lighthouse looked as though it had never been meant for anyone to use.

In fact, out in the water was the proof that on one night at least, the lighthouse had been dark. A wrecked cargo ship was lying on its side against a rocky shoal. From the looks of its bashed-up hull, the ship had been there for many years. And it had clearly met its end on the rocks in the shallow water.

Well, here I was at the end of the world—or what felt like it. The ring had brought me this far, and I could tell it wouldn't take me any farther. But where was Trevor? The only thing I could think was that he must be inside the lighthouse. Otherwise, what was I doing here?

Fog swirled tauntingly around me as I crept toward the lighthouse. The little barred window was too high for me to see into; I'd have to try the door.

I tiptoed up to the door and put a trembling hand on the iron latch. It creaked threateningly, but nothing else happened. I pushed the door open the tiniest crack.

And then it swept open in front of my face, and Vincent Graver stepped out toward me.

"So, Meg. We meet again," he said.

CHAPTER TEN

"H-hey, Vincent," I said tremblingly. "How are you doing?"

Vincent loomed over me, as pale and gray as a tombstone. His cavernous eyes stared down with dull, passionless hatred. I darted a glance down at his fingernails: yes, they were still pointed. So were his teeth, which made his smile rather . . . unwelcoming.

He stared coldly down at me. "I believe you have something of mine," he answered. "My ring."

"And I believe you have something of *mine*," I snapped. "My brother!"

"Perhaps we could effect a trade," Vincent said with an ugly leer. "You will be getting the worse end of the bargain, I fear. Your brother has been *most* difficult to deal with. Who would expect such behavior toward a former babysitter?"

"You monster!" I burst out. "If you've done anything to hurt Trevor, I'll—"

"I have done nothing to hurt your brother," Vincent cut in again. "He has only hurt himself with his foolish antics. Come in and see for yourself. But before I let you in, I would like to ask a favor. Please remove those disgusting necklaces and throw them into the ocean. I am afraid I really cannot let you into my home smelling like that."

Slowly I took off the three garlic braids and hurled them into the sea. I watched, biting my lip, as they bobbed merrily away into a wave. There went the only protective gear I had.

"Thank you *so* much." Vincent swept the door open again and gave me a bow of mocking courtesy. "After you, my dear," he said in the hollow voice that had always set my teeth on edge.

As I walked into the lighthouse I was very, very aware of the fact that Vincent was behind me.

Of course I was expecting a room straight out of a horror movie. Lots of tall, carved wooden chairs, skulls on the mantelpiece, an operating table, a few torture devices—that kind of thing. However, I'd forgotten that this was an old lighthouse, not an old castle.

The round room I walked into was so dark that at first I couldn't see anything at all. Then, gradually, I realized that its only furniture was a cou-

ple of wooden crates where furniture would usually be. Pittsy was perched on one of the crates, painting on some nail polish so industriously that she didn't even look up as I came in. There were a few dusty lifejackets hanging on the wall and a battered pair of oars leaning up against it, an old windbreaker on the floor, and some fishing nets rolled up nearby.

Trevor was crouched next to the nets. One of them had been used to tie his ankles. He rose and took a struggling step toward me, then stopped. The net was making it too hard for him to move.

"Trevor!" I cried. I rushed toward him and began untying the net. "Are you all right?"

Trevor nodded sturdily. I could see tear stains on his face, but he seemed much calmer than I would have been in his place. "I'm fine," he said, and stepped free from the tangled net. "I knew you would come to find me. But Meg, I hate this. Let's go home right now."

I had been frightened of Vincent until this— who wouldn't be?—but now I was furious. "You coward," I said through clenched teeth. "Tying up a little kid who couldn't possibly hurt you!"

Vincent smiled sardonically. "You would be surprised," he said. "I do not think my shins will ever recover from his kicking. As I said, I deemed it safer to secure him lest he do something that really angered me. I am a forgiving person, but even I have my limits."

"He was a *total* brat," Pittsy chimed in. "Why do you think I'm redoing my nails? It was, like, impossible to get him to sit down like a good boy!"

"Well, you don't have to worry about him anymore," I said bitingly. "Come on, Trev. We're going home."

"Not just yet," Vincent hissed. "First, the ring."

His icy hand grabbed at mine.

I thrust my hand behind my back. "Not just yet," I replied in the same hissing tone he had used. I was surprised at how steady my voice sounded. "You're not getting this ring until you tell me a few things. Why you didn't die when the sun hit you the last time I saw you. How you got back to Moose Island. What you've been—been living on since you got here."

For the briefest of seconds, Vincent's eyes flicked over to Pittsy. As if she sensed his attention, she looked up and held out one of her hands. Her nails were now neon pink. "Do you like this color, Victor?" she asked.

"It is fine," said Vincent distantly. "But I believe Meg has some more questions for me. I suppose she deserves an explanation after her persistence in hunting me down."

"*I* have a question," Trevor piped up. "Why does Kelly keep calling you Victor when your name is really Vincent?"

"I have many names, Trevor," said Vincent.

"Gee, you do?" Pittsy looked up from her nails again. "You mean because you're such an aristocrat?"

Again came the sardonic smile. "Exactly. Now, Meg, you wanted to know how—and, no doubt, why—I came back to this wretched little island."

"*Wretched* is a good word for it," Pittsy added. "It's the most boring place I've ever been in my life. Until I met you, Victor," she added gooily.

"I certainly would not have chosen to return," said Vincent to me. "Unfortunately, I had no choice in the matter. The instant the sun rose, I ducked under the water. When you so inconsiderately dropped the dirt from my coffin into the ocean—and that was *most* thoughtless of you—I was forced to take refuge in the wrecked ship outside this lighthouse."

"*What* dirt from *what* coffin?" demanded Pittsy, glancing up from her nails again. "What are you guys talking about?"

I stared at her in amazement. Did she really not know what kind of person Vincent was?

But Vincent was smiling at her. "It will all become clear in time, Kelly," he said. "You will see." He ran his tongue over his teeth in a particularly un-nice way, then turned back to me.

"The wrecked ship was not as uncomfortable as I had expected," he said. "And although I could not exactly sleep *in* the dirt from my coffin, I could at least sleep in the water that contained it. Unfortunately, the dirt eventually washed ashore," he added.

"That day on the public beach with Jack!" I suddenly remembered. "Some dark, weird-looking sand washed ashore. And right after that, there was a huge storm. Did that have something to do with you?"

Vincent bowed. "No doubt the island was having a slight reaction to my presence," he said. "The coffin dirt mixing with the sand, you know. Those in my family have often found that the weather becomes more violent in places where we appear."

"You mean, Moose Island has been trying to spit you out?"

"If you will. In any case, I would have had to return to the island eventually. My coffin was still here. As was my ring. And I need both of them."

"Well, of course you need the ring." Pittsy

smoothed her hair complacently. "You want to give it to me."

This time Vincent didn't even look at her. "The ring, as you have learned by now, confers second sight on its wearer," he told me. "It also brings bad luck to any wearer who is not its true owner. Have you experienced bad luck this summer, Meg?"

"You could call it that," I said dryly. "On top of seeing you again, I mean."

"Your rudeness displeases me," Vincent observed in a voice that made my spine crinkle with fear. Maybe I was acting *too* tough.

"Allow me to continue," he said. "Every member of my family owns a similar ring. We are given them at birth. Now, when our clan was scattered from our tiny village ten centuries ago—"

"By angry peasants or something, I suppose?" I broke in scornfully.

"Exactly." Vincent frowned at something none of us could see. "They were a crude bunch who could not understand our goals. The way they treated us was most unpleasant. Since their attack, we have been attempting to reunite with the help of our rings, which enable us to communicate with others wearing them."

Trevor was staring at Vincent in amazement.

"Ten centuries? You mean you're a thousand years old?" he asked.

"Much more than that, Trevor. Much more," said Vincent.

"I don't *get* this!" whined Pittsy.

"Your obtaining the ring made things somewhat difficult for me," Vincent went on. "Communication among the members of my family is essential for our survival. With the rings we are able to inform one another which regions are safe for our kind. Fortunately, wearing the ring for so long has given me a certain measure of second sight even when the ring is not on my finger. That is how I realized that the ring was in *your* possession. I had always removed it for sleeping, which I now realize was most unwise of me."

So I had been right. The ring *had* been in Vincent's coffin. That was how it had ended up in our canvas bag.

Again Vincent frowned at a troublesome memory. "But how to get the ring away from you was a problem," he said thoughtfully. "I followed you for a few days—in disguise, of course."

With a shudder, I remembered the bat I'd seen at the window on that stormy night, and the bat skeleton that had bitten me in the attic. "Where did that bat skeleton come from, anyway?" I asked suddenly.

"It was already there when I dropped in on your attic and found it. The poor, unfortunate creature must have died up there. I thought it would be amusing to try reanimating it. 'Bite bone to waken it,' my grandmother always used to tell me. Did I succeed?" he asked curiously.

"Kind of."

"That is excellent news. But I still could not discover a way to recover my ring. And then I had the great good fortune to meet Kelly." Vincent gave her one of his distant smiles. "Who volunteered to help me. And who, when she was unable to persuade you to give me the ring, had the idea of bringing your brother here in the hope that you would see reason."

"But you don't want the ring for *yourself*," Pittsy said eagerly. She set her bottle of nail polish down on the floor and walked over to Vincent. Gingerly she set her just-dry hand on his shoulder. "You want to give it to *me*. As a sign of your love. Right?"

Vincent eyed her in silence for a second. Then he brushed her hand off his shoulder as if it were a fleck of dust.

"Perhaps you should realize the truth now, Kelly," he said. "Let us say that I am not interested in you in the way you think I am. You appeal to me for reasons you may not have considered. And so, of course, do Meg and Trevor."

114

I didn't like the sound of that at *all*. "Just one more question," I said quickly. "Was that you following me on the beach last night?"

"Ah, yes. Your personal hygiene leaves something to be desired, I must say."

I ignored that. "Okay, just one *more* question. If the ring's supposed to bring me bad luck, why did it end up helping me? I mean, why did it show me how to find Trevor? Finding him was *good* luck, not bad."

"You surprise me," said Vincent. "Do you think walking into my home is good luck? For me, maybe, but not for you. *You* thought the ring was bringing you to your brother. But *I* think it was bringing you to me. Which one of us will prove right, I wonder?"

And he took a step toward me.

Now, suddenly, the realization of the danger we were in came over me in full force. Vincent wasn't going to agree to a pleasant little exchange of his ring for my brother. He was going to—

Pittsy interrupted my panicky thoughts. "Victor can I try the ring on now?" she asked. "I've been, like, waiting and waiting for this moment. Once I'm wearing the ring, is it okay for me to tell my parents about you? Because I don't think they'll want me going steady with you unless they meet you first. You know how parents—"

"Don't you *get* it, Kelly?" I burst out. "Vincent

is a *vampire!* He doesn't want to go steady with you! He just wants to drink your blood!"

Pittsy stared at me. Her mouth opened in horror. And then a cry of anguish burst from her lips.

"No way!" she screeched. "People don't drink the blood of people they *love!*"

"Actually, Kelly, Meg is quite right," said Vincent approvingly. "Even now I am feeling quite—thirsty. Will the three of you join me in a little snack?"

And he grabbed me by the throat.

I couldn't move. Vincent's hands were like steel. Slowly, terribly slowly, he brought me closer to those sharp, gleaming teeth. . . .

"Hey! Put my sister down!" said Trevor shrilly. He dashed over to the wall and picked up one of the oars leaning against it. Before Vincent could make a move, Trevor had crashed the oar down hard onto his head.

Vincent bellowed with pain and rage. He turned to beat away the oar—and that gave me the instant I needed to wriggle out of his grip. I snatched one of the fishing nets up off the ground. Maybe I could trap him that way!

But the ring on my finger caught against the net and got pulled off. Before I could move, it had skittered across the floor, straight toward Vincent.

"No!" I gasped. I threw myself across the floor after the ring. Who knew what awful powers Vincent would have once the ring was safely on his finger?

But before I could get there—and before Vincent could get there—Pittsy had picked it up and handed it to him.

"I *know* you're just teasing me," she said. "This *is* a going-steady ring, right? Now put it on my finger and stop being so jittery."

Vincent didn't reply. He slipped the ring onto his own finger. Then he grabbed Pittsy by the shoulder.

"One more bite," he said slowly. "One more bite is all it will take. Then, my dear, the two of us will take over this feeble town."

"But I don't *want* to take over this feeble town," Pittsy protested weakly. "I just want to go steady with you!"

"And so you shall. In a way, that is." Now Vincent opened his mouth. And his deadly, gleaming teeth began to close in on Pittsy's neck.

"Leave her alone!" I begged. I grabbed Vincent's cape and tried to pull him away, but he was too strong for me.

"Ouch!" Pittsy said in surprise. "Something's biting me!"

She *still* didn't get it.

"Leave her alone!" I screamed, and hurled myself onto Vincent's back. With a roar of rage he dropped Pittsy and spun around so violently that he threw me clear across the room.

"Meg!" Trevor said. "Are you all right?"

"And *you,* you vicious little brat!" Vincent thundered. Now it was Trevor's turn to be grabbed. "I'll take care of you, too!" There was an insane light in Vincent's eyes.

It was over. I was never going to reach Trevor in time. And when Vincent was all through with him, he would start in on me and Pittsy. . . .

Then came a sound none of us was expecting: the click of the front door opening. We all froze in our places.

And Jack peered in at us. "Meg?" he called, staring wide-eyed into the dark room. "I was out sailing, and I saw you come in here. You didn't come out, so I—"

"Run! Jack, run!" I shrieked. "Go and get the police! Don't you get into trouble, too!"

Instead, Jack pushed the front door open wider and stepped inside.

That was all it took.

A brilliant shaft of sunlight burst through the doorway and hit Vincent square in the face.

The unearthly howl of pain he made is something that still wakes me up at night.

"No! *No!*" Vincent screamed in agony. He

threw up his arm to shield his face from the brightness—but it was too late.

As we watched in horror Vincent's body began to shrink and shrivel. His arms turned into claw-like hanging things, and his legs collapsed under him. His cape folded in on itself and melted away. His skin dried up like leather until it was creased and ancient-looking, and his face changed into a grinning skull. Still the horrible shrieking came out of his mouth. Then it turned into a hoarse, croaking wheeze.

And then the wheezing noise stopped, too, and Vincent never made another sound.

It all happened in less than a minute. One second, Vincent was towering over us. Ten seconds later, a tiny, withered, dried-up clawed *thing* was writhing on the floor in front of us—and ten seconds after that, all that was left of Vincent was a pile of ashes.

"So that's what vampires do when the sun hits them," Jack said quietly.

But Pittsy had the last word, as usual. Gazing down at the heap of dust Vincent had become, she wailed, "My boyfriend! What have you done with my *boyfriend?*"

CHAPTER ELEVEN

"I hate to tell you this, Kelly,' I said, "but Vincent just isn't good boyfriend material."

"Especially *now*," Jack added, unnecessarily.

As if in answer, the red-stoned ring that had caused all the trouble suddenly rolled across the floor toward me. I picked it up and stuffed it into my pocket. Now that I knew its history, I never wanted to wear it again—but it didn't seem safe to leave it in the lighthouse, either. I'd have to figure out what to do with it later.

Trevor had come up to stand next to me during Vincent's transformation. Suddenly he drew a deep, shuddering breath and slipped his hand into mine. "Can we go home now?" he asked.

"Of course, Trevor," I said, and gave his hand a squeeze. "But I think Jack and I have to figure out what to do with—uh—Vincent first."

"Can't you just sweep him up?" Trevor asked.

Ugh! Who would hold the dustpan? "That's one idea," I said carefully, "but I think maybe we need to bury his ashes or something. I wonder where his coffin is. He said it was still on the island somewhere."

Pittsy had been silent during all of this. She was still staring in shock at the ashes on the floor. "His coffin?" she asked now. "There's something that looks kind of like a coffin on the second floor. He—" She gave a gulping sob. "He always told me it was a planter."

"I'll go up and check the second floor," Jack offered. He ran lightly up the stairs. "Yes, the coffin's up here," he called. "Can you give me a hand, Meg?"

"Sure. Trevor, why don't you come, too?" Just because Pittsy wasn't going to be a threat anymore didn't mean I wanted to leave Trevor alone with her.

"All my life I've wanted to see the inside of a lighthouse," Trevor said gloomily as we walked up the winding stairs, "and now that I'm seeing one, I hate it."

I knew what he meant. Under ordinary circumstances, the lighthouse's little round rooms would have been fun to explore. But the room we found on the second floor was as chilly and damp-looking and charmless as the room with Vincent's body in it.

Of course, a coffin goes a long way toward making a room less than cheerful.

"Is that where they put dead people?" Trevor whispered.

I put my arm around his shoulders. "Yes, it is, honey," I said. "But you don't have to worry about it. We're just going to leave Vincent's— uh—remains in it so . . . um . . . so the downstairs will be neat again."

With lots of bumping, scraping, and grunting, the three of us got the heavy coffin downstairs. Pittsy was still huddled on her crate when we walked in. She looked up dolefully.

"I sure hope you're not expecting *me* to touch that thing," she said, gesturing toward Vincent. "Because it just grosses me out! I'm not going *near* it!"

"We'll do it," grunted Jack as he set down his end of the coffin with a thud. "But shouldn't we wrap the ashes up in something before we put them in? In case they—you know—start moving or something"

"*What?*" asked Trevor and Pittsy in unison.

"Oh, Jack's just kidding." I gave him a warning glance. "That old windbreaker is the only thing, I guess. Let's kind of sweep the ashes up in it."

Silently and gingerly, and looking away as much as possible, the two of us swept Vincent's ashes up in the windbreaker. Then we wrapped a fishnet around the windbreaker like a rope, tied it fast, and dropped the bundle into the coffin.

"And I always felt sorry for my parents when they had to clean up cat throw-up!" I said. "Boy, I'm going to wash my hands five thousand times when we get home." With a shudder, I slammed down the top of the coffin. "Okay, that will hold him. Now, Trevor, let's get you home."

We closed the lighthouse door carefully behind us, and the four of us began walking back down the beach. The sun was beautifully warm on our backs, the ocean was a bright blue dotted with crisp little whitecaps. We hadn't had such nice weather in weeks.

"Wow, that was really heavy," Pittsy said as we walked along. "I guess my parents were right, Meg. Fourteen *is* too young to go steady. I feel kind of dumb," she added, to my surprise. "You know, I'm really starting to think that Victor, or Vincent, or whatever his stupid name was, was just *using* me! I think maybe he never loved me at all!"

I bit my lip. "I think you may be right about that, Kelly. It's too bad."

"It sure is! Plus, what's all this turning-me-into-a-vampire stuff?"

"Well, you see," said Jack carefully, "if a vampire bites you three times, it's supposed to turn you into a vampire, too. At least that's what the books say. But it's probably not true anyway."

124

"*He* said he'd bitten me only twice! But really it's already *been* three times! At least he kissed me three times, and it sure felt like bites! But maybe that was just part of his, you know, personal technique."

"Well," I said with distaste, because this was the *last* thing I felt like talking about, "maybe he kissed you three times but only bit you twice."

"Or maybe vampires aren't good at counting," Jack added so quietly that only I heard him.

"One thing's for sure," Pittsy said. "I'm not going to the Community Center anymore. You *never* meet anyone nice there."

About that, at least, Jack and I could totally agree with her.

For the rest of the walk home, we were all pretty quiet. What we'd all been through was just starting to sink in. It's tiring, fighting vampires. The fatigue creeps up on you.

When we finally reached Pittsy's house, she just stood there looking down at the ground.

"See you around?" I ventured halfheartedly.

"Uh-huh,' Pittsy answered just as halfheartedly. She dug her sneaker into the dirt. "Look, I'm really sorry about what happened. I didn't want to hurt Trevor or anything. I just wanted to help Victor. Vincent. *You* know."

"I know," I said quickly.

"Because, you know, I'm a very sensitive person, and if you've noticed, I like to help people as much as I can."

"I know," I said again.

"So anyway, see you around. And, uh, thanks. I mean, *you* aren't to blame for ruining my romance."

And with that, she walked up the driveway to her house.

"It's a slight improvement, but it's an improvement," I said to Jack as I watched Pittsy walk into her house. "Maybe she'll be less awful after this."

"And maybe dogs can learn to ski," said Jack dubiously. "What time is it, anyway?"

I checked my watch. "Wow, it's only three o'clock! I thought it was *way* later than that. I wonder if Mom and Dad are back from lunch yet."

But they weren't. The house was empty. Mom and Dad had probably decided to do some errands after lunch.

I looked at Trevor, and suddenly I was worried about him. What he had just gone through was much more traumatic than what Jack and I had just gone through. He's a very sensible kid and everything, but he *is* only seven.

"You know, Trev," I said, "it's been a long

126

time since you've had both me and Jack to boss around. What would you like to play?"

Trevor's face lit up. "You mean you'll *both* play with me?"

"Absolutely," I said, and Jack nodded.

"How about dinosaurs, then? We haven't played dinosaurs in a while. I'll be *Tyrannosaurus,* and Jack can be *Allosaurus,* and you can be some kind of little plant-eater that we chase around."

So I crouched down in my best plant-eating posture, and the three of us were dinosaurs until Mom and Dad came home at last.

CHAPTER 12

"Do you have the matches?" Jack asked.

"Yes. They're right here."

"Then I think we've got everything," said Jack. "Let's go!"

It was late afternoon. My parents had come home (they'd gone to a quilt exhibit after lunch) and taken Trevor for a walk.

Trevor was all back to normal now, and I knew he wouldn't tell Mom and Dad what had happened. "If you need to talk about it, talk to me," I had said to him just before my parents came back. "It would only make them confused."

Trevor had nodded wisely. "Grownups never understand about things like that," he said. "Like Mom never understands why I want a pet ostrich, either. Anyway, what would I talk to you *about*? It's all over now, right?"

I could see he was feeling better.

Anyway, after Mom and Dad and Trevor had left, Jack and I had looked at each other. "You know we have to go back, don't you?" Jack said at last.

"I guess so. We've got to get rid of Vincent for good this time."

So that's what we were getting ready to do now.

"Okay, let's go," said Jack. "We want to set sail before it starts getting dark."

Our plan needed Jack's boat, which was still moored on the beach outside the lighthouse. We were going to dump Vincent's body into the ocean, sail to a tiny island Jack knew about, and burn the coffin.

The ring, by the way, was still in my pocket. We hadn't been able to figure out what to do with it.

"We could burn it along with the coffin," I suggested to Jack as we began the walk back to the lighthouse.

"We could," he answered doubtfully, "but it seems a little dangerous to me. What if burning the ring releases some kind of communication ray? Bang! All of a sudden, hundred of vampires would be on their way here to find out what was going on. Of course, that would be sort of an adventure—"

"Not the kind I want," I said hastily. "Let's forget about burning it."

"We could just put it back in with Vincent's ashes," Jack said. "It is his, after all. Was his, I mean. That might be the fairest thing to do."

"That's fine with me, as long as *you* put it in his ashes."

There was a pause.

"I'm sure we'll think of something," said Jack.

When we reached the lighthouse, we both hesitated at the front door for a second. "I wish we could see in the window," I whispered.

"Nothing could have happened," Jack said scornfully, but I noticed that he was whispering also. For some reason that actually made me feel braver. I pushed the door open, and we walked inside.

The coffin was lying in the same place we'd left it, and it was still closed. Was it my imagination, though, or had the rocks Jack put on top of it moved ever so slightly? Had something jiggled them a little—a knocking from inside the coffin, perhaps?

I gathered up my courage, strode over to the coffin, pushed the rocks away, and opened it. Then Jack and I stared in silence at the ashes inside.

"It's hard to believe they were ever scary," said Jack.

It really was. But something about the ashes was still bothering me.

"Doesn't it look as though he—they—uh, the ashes have moved around since we closed the coffin?" I asked, and pointed. "I mean, weren't they down at *this* end, not that end? You don't think Vincent could be rearranging himself and coming back to life, do you?"

"Oh, I'm sure he isn't," said Jack quickly. "Anyway, let's get the coffin out to the boat."

There was more bumping and grunting while we lugged the heavy coffin outside and dragged it into the boat, but at last it was aboard. "Let's get a few of the rocks, too," said Jack. "We can use them to weigh down the ashes." So we got three of the biggest rocks and lugged them aboard, too. Then we pushed the boat into the water and hopped in ourselves.

"I guess your sailing lessons came in handy after all," I remarked as we set sail. There was a brisk breeze now, and the boat moved quickly through the water. Jack was only acting a little bit captainly, I was glad to see.

"I know I haven't gotten to see you much this summer," he answered. "It's just—well, I've got to fit in with the kids at school during the year, you know. I can't just goof off all summer."

So Jack thought seeing me was goofing off? I

felt a little wistful at the thought, but I didn't say anything. The summer was only halfway over, and we had lots of summers ahead of us. Maybe the thing for me to do was start learning to sail myself. . . .

"I think we're deep enough now." Jack's voice broke into my thoughts. "Time for old Vincent here to take a little dip."

"Jack, that's disgusting!" I protested. But I opened the coffin and pulled out the scrunched-up windbreaker. Then we each unwrapped one sleeve, tucked some rocks inside, and wrapped it up again.

"Ready?" Jack asked.

I nodded. We each picked up one end of the weighted-down bundle. Then we held it over the water.

"I'll count," I said. "One."

Good-bye, Vincent.

"Two."

Don't ever come back, now.

"Two and a half."

"This isn't water pollution, is it?" Jack suddenly asked.

"I don't think so. I think bodies are biodegradable. Sometimes they bury people at sea, you know. *Three!*"

And we hurled the body into the water with all the strength we had.

The bundle of windbreaker, net, rocks, and Vincent hit the water cleanly and sank without a sound. A few bubbles rose up from the spot and disappeared. Then all we could see were the gently lapping waves.

I let out a big sigh. "That's over with," I said slowly.

"Are you sad?" Jack asked in amazement.

"Well, not exactly. It's just that it wasn't Vincent's fault he was a vampire. I bet he hated being one, sometimes. Never getting to settle down, always having to hunt for blood, sleeping in a coffin . . ."

"I didn't hear him complaining," Jack said dryly. "Anyway, he'll never sleep in his coffin again. See that little island over there? That's the one I was telling you about."

It was a tiny spot, hardly an island at all. A thin strip of sand gave it a narrow beach, and there were three or four stunted trees at one end. A few seagulls were wheeling around overhead. That was all.

"How did you ever find this place?" I asked as Jack brought the boat to shore.

"My sailing instructor brought the class here once. Some rich summer people own it, but they don't do anything with it, he told us. I mean, what could they do here? It's not even big enough for a one-room shack!"

But it was big enough for burning a coffin. When the boat was safely aground, we lifted out the coffin once more and put it down on the sand. ("That will keep the fire from spreading," Jack said.)

"Are you ready?" I asked. And I took the box of matches out of my pocket.

I lit a match and held it out toward the coffin. Then I suddenly blew it out.

"What's the matter?" asked Jack.

"This isn't arson, is it?" I said.

"Arson? Burning a vampire's coffin? If the fire department knew about it, they'd thank us for saving them the job."

"Okay. Just checking." I lit another match and touched it to the edge of the coffin.

Whoooosh! A sheet of fire leaped out so fast that Jack and I barely got out of the way without being singed. Clouds of foul-smelling smoke poured into the air, and in seconds the whole coffin was ablaze with white-hot flames.

Overhead, the seagulls were shrieking their dismay. And it *was* a pretty dramatic fire. The varnish on the outside of the coffin must have been flammable, because the flames didn't die down for a long, long time.

Finally, though, they'd settled down into a nice pile of coals with a pleasant glow of warmth—

just the thing for a crisp summer afternoon in Maine. The ocean was calm, and the sky was even bluer than it had been earlier that day. Even nature was happy that Vincent was gone.

"We should have brought some marshmallows," Jack said suddenly.

"Yuck! Are you crazy?" I shrieked. "Marshmallows cooked over *coffin* coals?"

"Oh, come on," Jack scoffed. "Coals are coals."

"No, they're not. Jack, that smoke's got vampire germs in it!"

"Well, that would probably make the marshmallows taste better," Jack said with an evil twinkle in his eye. "It would give them a—"

"Stop! Stop! I'm not listening!" I jumped to my feet.

And as I did Vincent's ring rolled out of my pocket onto the sand.

For a moment Jack and I stared down at it. "I forgot all about this," I said. "Should we burn it after all?"

"Sure. I guess that's the safest thing."

I bent down to pick up the ring.

Suddenly, from out of nowhere, a huge bird swooped down, grabbed the ring in its claws, and flew away.

"What was that?" I gasped, with a lurch of terror in my stomach.

Jack had gone pale. "It—it must have been a seagull," he said, not quite meeting my eyes. "Probably thought we had food or something."

But what a strange-looking seagull it had been! Black, with such weirdly shaped wings and such an odd, loopy way of flying. Almost like—

"Almost like a bat," I said in a whisper.

ANN HODGMAN is a former children's book editor and the author of over twenty-five children's books, including the bestselling *There's a Batwing In My Lunchbox, My Babysitter Is a Vampire*, and the Lunchroom series. In addition to humorous fiction for children, she has written teen mysteries and non-fiction for reluctant readers. She is also a writer for *The Big Picture*, a series of educational posters distributed in schools nationwide. She lives with her husband and two children in Washington, Connecticut.

JOHN PIERARD is best known for his illustrations for Isaac Asimov's *Science Fiction Magazine, Distant Stars*, the bestselling My Teacher Is An Alien series, *My Babysitter Is a Vampire*, and several books in the Time Machine series. He lives in Manhattan.